A Window Into Yesterday

A compilation of 27 fiction short stories

Mike Henry Tkachuk

A Window Into Yesterday

These short stories are purely fictional. Although in some of these stories, the plot bears a modicum of fact, it has been embellished significantly to generate more interest. The names of characters are fictional, and any resemblance to real characters is purely coincidental.

Mike Henry Tkachuk

Previous publications:

Poetry, My Obsession

Perspective Reflections in Rhyme

tellwell

Tellwell Talent
www.tellwell.ca

ISBN
978-0-2288-6978-8 (Hardcover)
978-0-2288-6977-1 (Paperback)
978-0-2288-6979-5 (eBook)

I dedicate this book to my wife, Dolores. She has stood by me and encouraged me to pursue my passion for writing. I am grateful for her patience and understanding throughout this process of writing and publishing my third book.

Table of Contents

ANIMALS

Song of Freedom

As autumn fades into winter, sub-zero temperatures cap the wildlife's water supply until the spring thaw. Waterfowl purposely move to a warmer climate until their water resource returns. The Canada goose is just one such species greatly affected by this anomaly of nature.

The Canada goose (Branta Canadensis) is a large wild goose genus with a black head and neck, white cheeks, white under its chin, and a brown torso. These birds are native to the Arctic and temperate regions of North America, and their migration occasionally reaches northern Europe. When the water turns to ice in November, instinct drives them south to a warmer climate for the winter. When they return in the spring, they seek to nest close to freshwater locations. Here a mother goose chose to lay the eggs that produced a golden boy she named Brant.

The adventure of Brant, a young male goose with a unique penchant for autonomy, is remarkable. Hatched in the northern part of Manitoba in the early spring, he shared a nest with seven siblings.

This young gosling displayed early signs of maturity and independence from the onset. The moment Brant and his siblings received their eviction notice from the nest, Brant chose to explore the world on his own. One day, while Brant and his siblings were marching to the lake behind their mother in military fashion, Brant checked out a frog that went bouncing across the grass nearby. As they approached the lake, his attention was diverted to a snake wriggling through the weeds in the swamp.

By July, Brant had matured enough to try out his wings. When he felt they were strong enough to lift him off the ground, he flapped them several times and suddenly found himself airborne. This new experience was a glorious and promising day of independence. The newfound freedom offered countless choices he could only envision in his dreams. The possibilities were endless.

As October approached and migration was imminent, the leader designated a junior gander from that flock to scout the land and find harvested fields for food. The task included detecting any danger that might befall the gaggle from unsuspected enemies. The responsibility fell on Brant, who felt honoured to be chosen. The flight south required much stored energy. The grain left behind on the field by the combines would serve them well for the journey.

When Brant discovered a field ready for feeding, he signalled all the other geese to a meal. In unison, the entire flock lifted off the lake and followed the leader to the area for their repast. Reaching their target, they circled the field twice. Since they saw no wild animal predators below, the flock descended for the feast. Brant continued serving as the lookout for the gaggle while they gorged on the grain. Coyotes, wolves, or fox on the prowl often looked for a meal, and a goose dinner would fit the bill nicely.

As Brant kept circling the field, he suddenly spied unusual movement in nearby tall grass. Something was crawling surreptitiously toward the flock. As he descended for a closer look at the intruder, a goose-hunter suddenly stood up, pointed his shotgun, and fired. Brant, startled by the gunfire, veered to one side. At that moment, a buckshot pellet tore into his right wing and splintered a bone. The pain was excruciating, causing him to give a loud honk to warn the others. At the sound of the alarm and perhaps the loud noise of gunfire, the entire flock lifted off the field and returned to the lake. As for the scout, his broken wing could not keep him airborne for much longer.

Brant flew some distance with the injury until the unbearable pain finally forced him to land. He came down with a thud on solid ground, stunned but alive. With his now broken wing dragging along, Brant struggled through the tall grass, searching for water and safety from predators. He worked his way through the dense vegetation in search of safety for some time. Suddenly, he realized providence had just cancelled his plans to fly south. As with most plans, you never know how they will turn out until it's too late.

Meanwhile, a coyote crawled through the bush in a distant grove of trees, looking for a morsel. The sound of the shotgun blast had startled the animal for a moment. Nearing the edge of the woods, he had spied the goose coming in for a landing. Then when the thud came of Brant landing heavily on the ground, the coyote crawled slyly toward the spot where the goose had landed.

Fortunately for Brant, a conservation officer was checking hunting permits as it was hunting season. He heard the gunshot and saw the goose gliding down near him in the meadow. The hunter was unaware the goose was hit and did not search to retrieve it. Brant was quickly found and captured since the injury disabled its flying ability. The game warden placed the injured bird in a cage and drove to a nearby town's veterinarian.

The doctor splintered the damaged wing and returned Brant to the officer. The goose was caged and transported to a nearby farmer who offered refuge to injured animals. There it would be cared for until it could fly again. The farmer had a fenced yard where all the domestic fowl were kept and fed. They were all herded into their pens in the evening, safe from roaming predators.

One cold and cloudy day, the world turned white as snowflakes blanketed the land. Instinct told him migration would begin with the first snowfall, so he kept looking skyward for signs of the flock's departure. Then he noticed his family winging their way south in vee formation. He longed to be with them and not cooped up among these domestics. Yet this predicament was far better than becoming a snack for some hungry wolf. He bid them all a fond farewell and a safe journey with a loud honk and a wave of his good wing. As they faded into the horizon, he wondered if he would ever see them again.

The winter months were sad and lonely for him. He missed his clan immensely. Yet, being alive and feeling less pain each day in his fractured wing comforted him. A cordial rapport developed between Brant and the domestics through the winter months. The domestic flock willingly shared their food and water with the stranger in their midst.

In March of the following year, Brant's wound had healed enough to attempt a liftoff. He tried flapping the damaged wing and felt no pain. What a relief it was to find he could fly once more!

One morning, he heard that old familiar sound of honking geese. Looking skyward, the same flock he missed so dearly during his recovery had returned. He spread his wings, gave them a few flaps, and gloriously lifted himself off the ground.

Rising above the fence, he circled the farm twice, let out a great honk of gratitude to his guardians, and rejoined his lost siblings. There was much rejoicing at the reunion!

Brant's struggle arose from his song of freedom. It was about finding his purpose in life, overcoming fear, and standing up for noble causes bigger than his own. Here the outcome ended favourably, and despite the danger, he continued to serve as a scout and lookout for his family.

A Potential Winner

Pamela, a kennel owner in Newfoundland, fell in love with an adorable little female canine the day the dog was born. She was a cute Pekingese puppy from a litter of five. Six weeks after the litter was born, Pamela sold them all but two. The female's registered name was Sunrise Over Corner Brook, but the owner lovingly nicknamed her Sunny. She would be the pride and joy of Pam's life, and she hoped her dog would be crowned Best of Show at the Westminster Kennel Club Dog Show one day.

When most other puppies found new adopted families, Pamela was grooming Sunny for greatness at home. The puppy kept company with her one-eyed brother, Sparky, whom no one wanted. Unfortunately, while roughhousing with her brother one day, she sat on Sparky, causing his eye to pop out. Since then, potential customers have kept shying away from adopting him. But Sunny was happy, for she had someone to play with all day.

After grooming and pampering Sunny for nearly a year, Pamela took her puppy to the veterinarian to get her shots. The doctor gave her some disappointing news. Sunny was perfect in every way but one. She had crooked teeth. This anomaly meant disaster for someone planning to take the animal on a circuit for show. Pamela had a choice to make. She could keep the puppy as a pet or sell her. The decision to let her go was difficult, for she had grown fond of the little girl puppy.

Soon after, Pamela received a phone call from a Winnipeg couple looking to buy a female Pekingese pup. Pamela told them about Sunny, a female in the breed they wanted, but the dog was already one year old. She explained the circumstances for the delay in selling her and assured the buyers the dog was perfect in every other aspect but crooked teeth.

Since there was such a great distance to Winnipeg, the problem of transporting Sunny halfway across Canada arose. The other problem was the reputation of the buyers. Breeders usually choose not to sell their puppies to someone without background knowledge of that person. They prefer to sell their dogs to good homes where they will be well treated. The onus was on the buyer to assure the breeder of their ability to provide proper care and treatment for the animal.

Jack and Rhonda, the couple from Winnipeg, recently lost their eighteen-year-old registered female Pekingese dog. Near its eighteenth birthday, pancreatic cancer agonized the animal. The veterinarian recommended euthanizing the dog to alleviate its suffering. Pam was amazed at the animal's fantastic longevity, for small dogs rarely live for eighteen years. This information assured her that a caring family was adopting Sunny. But the family lived halfway across the country. She wondered how Sunny would fare travelling there all alone.

The owner resolved the transportation problem quickly with a few brilliant ideas and put her plan into action. Pam placed the dog in a small crate, brought it to the airport, and directed them to ship it to Winnipeg. She reminded the carrier to provide food and water for the dog once they reached Toronto. The couple had agreed to pick Sunny up at the airport in Winnipeg.

When the dog arrived in Winnipeg, Jack and Rhonda claimed Sunny and brought her home. The moment Rhonda set her eyes on the puppy, she fell in love with the little tyke. It was the cutest Pekingese she had ever seen. It was light brown with dark strands of black hair on either side of her head, framing her pretty face. Rhonda now understood why Pamela was keeping her for a show dog. The bonding between Rhonda and Sunny increased, and soon the dog became very protective of her. She distrusted every visitor that arrived at the doorstep. Now, the new place became her home, and every doorbell ring would elicit growls and barks.

When the occupants turned in for the night, Rhonda asked Jack if he had set the security alarm for the night. He could not remember programming the alarm, so he went down the stairs. On checking, he had forgotten to set the signal and did so.

At approximately one in the morning, a loud bang at the front door aroused the family. The pounding continued several times, and then came a loud crash. The hinges let go, and the door plunged to the floor. The alarm shattered the stillness of the air and brought Sunny to the front of the house, growling and barking unceasingly. Now awake, Jack and Rhonda emerged from their bedroom, curious to see what caused all the commotion. Suddenly, Sunny leaped down the stairs in a flash, with teeth bared, ready to attack the intruder.

The occupants immediately realized this was a home invasion. The noise of the alarm, as well as Sunny's growling and bearing of her teeth, frightened the intruder. As he retreated from the house, his jacket fell, and in desperation to get away, he abandoned it on the lawn.

Meanwhile, the family wondered what had happened to Sunny. They looked everywhere, under the bed, in the closet, but nowhere could they locate her. They ran over to the front door and saw Sunny dragging someone's jacket in from the outdoors. That day, Sunny became a hero and a winner in her class.

A minute after the house alarm had sounded, the phone rang. An employee from the Alarm Company called to find out if they needed the police. When told of the home invasion, the police were called and were at their doorstep in five minutes.

After the police arrived, they picked up the coat Sunny retrieved and drove around the neighbourhood looking for the perpetrator but to no avail. However, from the gas receipt in the jacket pocket, the culprit was apprehended and charged with home invasion.

Everyone loves a winner. That is just how the world is. Although Sunny's teeth disqualified her from the kennel club circuit, her teeth won her recognition in Jack and Rhonda's hearts.

Unconditional Love

The bonding between a dog and a human is fascinating but challenging to explain. A family without a dog is like a house without an alarm system. Both are virtually indispensable. Is it any wonder that humans in our society gave dogs the nickname *man's best friend*? In Canada, dogs are the epitome of unconditional love. Therefore, many families own such a pet.

Several months after Ron and Donna Smith exchanged marriage vows, they wanted a pet for their new home. There was always a pet dog in each of their parents' homes, and they missed having one around. They knew that adopting a dog meant having to say goodbye to it within ten or fifteen years. They knew how emotional it would be to see it go. But that was not a deterrent, for dogs bring so much joy and happiness to a caring family.

When the couple decided to acquire a pet, the hunt was on for a lap dog. Almost a year went by before they found the specific breed they wanted. It was two days before Christmas day and just one week before Donna's birthday when an opportunity arose to acquire a pet they were seeking.

Ron and Donna received some interesting information about their new dog at the time of purchase. The six-week-old female Pekingese puppy, Kia, was the most diminutive sibling of the litter, weighing only six pounds. Dog breeders often refer to these small Pekingese dogs as sleeves. The name comes from ancient times when emperors carried them in their sleeves. Her siblings always kept Kia from the kibble bowl at the kennel until they had their fill. Yet, she did not growl or snap at them when pushed away from the food. After they left, she would devour whatever remained in the bowl.

When New Year's Eve celebrations began, a strong bond had formed between Donna and Kia. From then on, the puppy became Donna's dog. Within days, it became a veritable and indispensable member of the family.

Kia did not bark, nor did she whimper. At three months of age, there still were no audible sounds coming from her. Her adopted family wondered whether their pet was born mute or whether her silence was merely a result of delayed maturation—a late bloomer. They reasoned that if she were mute, she would lack the qualities required of a watchdog. Likewise, the problem of maintaining a clean house was an issue. How would she let the family know if she needed to go outdoors? Training is necessary to maintain a hygienic environment in the home.

It may seem that house-training a young pup is the owner's responsibility. Oddly enough, however, pets seem to train the family rather than vice versa. When nature calls, dogs will usually stand by the door, whimper or bark, and wait for the owner to let it out. After several trials and occasional mishaps, it successfully trains its owner to open the door at its beckoning in acquiescing to the pet's wishes. Henceforth, this will become a daily routine. Kia did this. She would stand by the door and wait. However, not a sound came out of her while she waited desperately to get outdoors.

When a visitor arrived at the family's door, an ordinary dog would growl and bark at the stranger. Not Kia! She just looked up at the stranger and wagged her tail. The family wondered whether Kia would ever bark. She did not seem to have those character traits prevalent in an average dog determined to protect its territory and family at the risk of its own life. There were no loud alert barks, no growls, not even snarls when a stranger appeared in the doorway. The family wondered whether a battery-operated training gizmo existed to teach the young pup to bark. This notion, however, was never pursued.

Their concerns soon abated and died. One evening, Ron and Donna went to bed at the usual midnight hour following the eleven o'clock news. Kia slept at the foot of the bed, also as expected. Before turning off the lights, Kia would crawl up along Donna's side for a goodnight belly rub. After her belly rub, she returned to the foot of the bed. When Donna turned off the lights, everyone drifted off into dreamland.

At about three o'clock in the morning, a sudden chilling scream pierced the stillness of the night, causing Ron to sit up abruptly, expecting disaster. The sound seemed to emanate from Donna's side of the bed. Later that morning, he discovered that Donna was having a nightmare in which a giant mouse was attacking her. Ron knew about Donna's dreaded fear of mice and understood her reactions. This nightmare caused Donna to let out an ear-shattering scream that woke up everyone in the house, including the dog.

Much to everyone's surprise, the dog let out a bark, usually befitting that of a Rottweiler. Then came another and another just as loud. Kia barked without ceasing for what seemed like an hour. Donna picked up Kia in her arms, trying desperately to comfort and encourage her to stop barking. It was a workday, and Kia was keeping everyone awake.

However, oblivious to their concerns about sleep, the dog kept barking. Eventually, the frequency of barks decreased and then finally ceased altogether. Then the growls began and continued for at least another half hour, then silence. After the noises stopped, everyone went back to bed until the alarm clock rang. Both were yawning and tired in the morning. One thing was now inevitable: much to their surprise and delight, Kia was not mute.

Once she realized she had a voice and its effectiveness, there was no stopping her. From then on, every strange noise she heard evoked a bark. A creaking house during the winter months brought many alarming barks at all hours. This noise irritated the family, especially in the wee hours of the morning. However, the family was thrilled that Kia could emit an alarming bark. Should a burglar ever enter the house, she was ready to apprise the family of the intrusion.

Donna enjoyed the company of this furball immensely. As with most animals, soon medical problems arose. Early in her life, the veterinarian diagnosed Kia with a medical condition called epilepsy. With medication, the disorder was relatively mild and controllable. Her attacks occurred in regular three-month intervals and always created a state of fear and apprehension in Kia. When that happened, Donna picked her up and calmed her anxiety in a reassuring tone and eased much of Kia's fears. As time went on, Kia developed a routine. She would run to Donna for comfort whenever she sensed a seizure coming on. This response became a ritual in the family.

From tooth extraction to a gall stone operation, many years went by. At seventeen years of age, Kia developed pancreatitis and required a special diet for her condition. However, this disorder worsened to where Kia was experiencing extreme pain and discomfort. The contentious issue now was what they should do about it? The veterinarian's advice was to put her to sleep and avoid further suffering.

The family faced a grave decision. To have her just a few more days meant putting her through more pain and suffering, or they could take the veterinarian's advice and have her euthanized. The mere thought of losing Kia clouded Donna's eyes with a hazy sadness. Although tears of reality fell down her cheeks like rain, Donna reluctantly ended Kia's suffering. Standing by her wonderful pet, her heart at the breaking point, she watched the veterinarian inject the lethal dose of death into her precious Kia. With what seemed like a second, Kia let out a last gasp of air, her body went limp, and she was gone. Donna felt a part of her body tearing away.

Later that day, the veterinarian sent Kia's body for cremation. The incurable medical condition that caused her great suffering, pain and discomfort was alleviated and no longer caused her any more grief.

Yet, notwithstanding all of Kia's medical problems, the trials and tribulations that Donna experienced with Kia did not mitigate the loss of her precious pet. It was devastating! Donna requested in her will that upon her death, the urn of Kia's ashes would rest at her feet inside the coffin. Just as Kia always slept at the foot of the bed when she was alive, she would be resting there at Donna's feet for eternity.

Animals mean so much to humans in life. The problems of greed and hatred have resulted in many separations in our culture. But there is one thing we have in our lives we can depend on wholeheartedly. It is a dog that loves us unconditionally, every day, ever faithful to the end.

The Altruistic Intruder

Domestic cats are warm and cuddly; still, many people fear them. Only true cat lovers revere these playful animals. Their agility, power, strength, and mysterious nature have endeared them to people since the beginning of civilization. As pets, they quickly adapt to their environment and household routine.

Oscar, a domestic feline, can dispute that claim, for he struggled to settle into his new digs with his owner, Jed.

At eighteen, Jed's mother and father had died in a horrific automobile accident. His uncle Greg became responsible for Jed until he reached the legal age of twenty-one. His uncle's wife, Mary, died of cancer several years earlier, and he chose to remain single since then. Jed became the only close relative of Greg's and the inheritor of Greg's estate when Greg died. Although fortune fell into his lap, Jed seemed to lack something, making him unsettled and miserable. Finally, boredom got to him! In desperation, he sold the house in the small town where he lived and moved to the city.

Jed, a bachelor, and Oscar, a Cheshire cat, moved into a one-bedroom apartment in Toronto's sprawling metropolis. The change was drastic as they moved from a three-bedroom bungalow to a one-bedroom apartment. The bright lights and the hustle and bustle of city life made their move so alluring; he was confident his doldrums would vanish. Yet, the fast and exciting pace which drew them there seemed elusive. A sea of a million hearts surrounded them, yet boredom and loneliness engulfed them.

Their first night in the new home seemed long and arduous; interruptions were many. Jed's two-hour interval washroom visits, constant droning of city traffic, and ambulance sirens piercing the midnight air kept their sleep at a minimum. At eight in the morning, Oscar searched for the litter box. Awakening in a strange house disoriented him until he remembered where he lived.

By three in the afternoon, Oscar felt hungry. The Purina diet was adequate but paled in taste to the delicious flavour of his country-mouse food. With a litany of meows, he pleaded for Jed's attention. "Either feed me or let me out," was his appeal. Oscar knew how to obtain food in the wild without too much difficulty, but the challenge was enormous here in this vast city. He envisioned a varmint near the garbage bins outdoors that could yield a tasty morsel. However, Jed either ignored his pleas or had something on his mind that commanded his attention.

Oscar's immediate goal was to convince Jed how imperative it was for a cat to explore the outdoors! Jed knew cats are carnivores, always on the hunt. Oscar appeased his frustration by replaying the same old refrain in his mind that kept him happy and content in his previous home: "In the country, I can roam at will; it's the hunt that gives me a thrill!"

Suddenly, a knock at the door brought Oscar back to reality. This intrusion conjured up a brilliant thought in his mind. He envisioned slipping by this visitor when the door opened and making a break for the outdoors. However, like all excellent plans, some go awry. Getting out of the room was a no-brainer, but a five-story apartment building presented a significant problem. How would he accomplish the next phase of this venture? How would he get out of this building to find a mouse in this concrete sea? That was his dilemma!

When Jed opened the door, there stood an attractive young lady holding a snow-white, rhinestone-collard Persian cat in her arms. Oscar almost did a double somersault until he realized there were no athletic qualities in him. The young lady introduced herself to Jed as Penelope from the apartment next door. She heard that Jed had a handsome young cat and was familiar with their habits. That immediately grabbed Oscar's attention. The purpose of her visit was still a mystery, but he quickly took a liking to her.

The mystery was quickly solved when Penelope mentioned that she ran short of food for her cat, and she asked whether Jed could spare a cup. Since it was Sunday evening and most retail stores were closed, Jed offered her a bag of Oscar's food in a neighbourly fashion. He was certain Oscar wouldn't mind sharing some of his dry vittles with a stranger. Oscar didn't care! There were suddenly essential things craving his attention.

Then, Penelope asked if Jed could cat-sit for her when work called her out of the city for several days. She indicated that her employment as a flight attendant takes her away from home regularly, and she needed someone to look after her cat when she is away. Until the present, her mother always did that for her, but she moved into a nursing home and could no longer help her. It took just two seconds for Jed to respond and assure her that he would be glad to assist her. Wow! Oscar could not believe his ears. This city life was showing signs of action. By now, he had forgotten all about the hunger and lack of sleep. Just meeting a new friend was so exciting! Living those nine lives was now an immediate goal.

Early the following week, Penelope and her cat returned.

"Please take good care of Frederick for me while I am gone," she pleaded.

"Oh no, it can't be!" cried Oscar. "Why couldn't it have been Frederica?"

It crushed Oscar's heart. Little did he realize how his life would suffer living with a male Persian cat.

Freddy was a well-manicured cat, but stuffy and snobbish as one can be! He exuded an aura of egotism that conveyed the condescending message of "I am so far above you; you would need a helicopter to reach me! I will talk to you if I must, but don't expect me to adopt any of your redneck ways." This attitude of arrogance persisted until Penelope returned. But that situation was about to change.

Oscar noticed that Jed would be away most evenings whenever Penelope was in the city. He would dress up in his best attire and leave for several hours. Oscar assumed Jed had found suitable employment and was going for work. One day, Oscar discovered the real reason Jed was away those times. He was going on dates with Penelope. The two had fallen in love and were planning a wedding.

Since Jed had no family, Penelope's family took charge of all the arrangements. They had a fall wedding surrounded by gorgeous autumn leaves! After the church service, the bridal party drove to a nearby park within city limits for a photo session. Penelope's family and guests proceeded to the banquet hall for the reception. Several hundred were in attendance, including Oscar and Freddy, who had been neglected that day.

After the wedding, all four moved to a small town near the city. Oscar was so delighted by the move all he could say was, "I could live here, Freddy!"

Still thinking about the hunt, it was the most jubilant comment that day. For Oscar, a country cat, no matter where he would go or what he did, Oscar would always be country. But Freddy, with his nose pointed to the moon, stifled the nasty comments he so desperately wanted to share about country life. As he persevered with Freddy's self-seeking behaviour, Oscar remembered Jed's brilliant adage that snobs are insecure and lack confidence in themselves and their abilities. The knowledge gave Oscar another brilliant idea that at first ended in a catastrophe. He invited Freddy to go tomcatting with him one night. That proved to be a disaster! Freddy's snobbish attitude drove all the females away.

However, Oscar noticed a slight change in Freddy's demeanour as the days progressed. He was slowly slipping into mediocrity, allowing his stuffiness to dissipate. The transformation is gradual for cats and such small animals, for they display so much independence and dignity. Cats, unlike dogs, demand acceptance on their terms, proving Freddy was right to form.

All the credit goes to Penelope, who no longer spent hours combing, pampering, and keeping Freddy on a pedestal. There were now daily household chores to perform and employment commutes. There was no time to indulge Freddy; he had to fend for himself. As Freddy became more independent, he gained self-confidence and relied less on Penelope.

All the females were paying more attention to Freddy at the next dating venture. When his character changed, so did his popularity! The personality change was such a metamorphosis that all Oscar could say was, "Mwow!"

Eventually, Freddy and Oscar became the best of friends. They would go mouse-hunting together whenever they pleased. They went on the prowl at night, tomcatting and having a great time. The loneliness and boredom Jed and Oscar experienced in the city had lifted like the noonday fog.

Unlike the two cats, Jed and Penelope chose an alternate route to make their marriage last. They knew marriage demands love, respect, and nurture. The couple did not try to change the other into being the person of their design. That attempt takes on the form of manipulation, tricks, shaming and blaming. They maintained their practice of individualism, and it drew them closer together. They built one of the greatest marriages that the world has ever known.

Dream Speak

As we lay our souls to rest each night, the trials of the day begin to fade. Out of the darkest recesses of our mind emerge strange dreams that point the way to a better day. If they appear unrealistic at first, give them a chance to linger awhile, and they will come to fruition. At least, Donald and Juanita did that when they lost their family pet one summer day.

Don and Juanita owned an adorable toy poodle named Kimba. This elegant female loved to fly over, under and through obstacles with grace. Watching her feats took one's breath away. She was well-groomed because Juanita would take Kimba to a nearby groomer who would care for her coat and trim her nails. Whenever the toy poodle arrived home after being groomed, she would prance around the house like a proud celebrity showing off her accomplishments and beauty.

On a Thursday morning in August, Kimba suddenly became ill. She could not hold down any food she ate. Don and Juanita took the poodle to the veterinarian, hoping to restore her health. Sadly, the vet diagnosed her with Canine parvovirus. This illness can lead to fever, lethargy, vomiting, diarrhea, dehydration, and weight loss. This parvo is another highly contagious virus that infects dogs who encounter the fecal matter of a sick dog. It spreads quickly but is hard to kill once it attacks a dog's internal organs. The vet treated Kimba with plenty of fluids, electrolytes, and secondary infection prevention, but to no avail. Kimba died at the clinic.

Juanita's eyes flooded with tears when she got the tragic news. She was devastated and wondered where Kimba encountered the fecal matter that caused her demise. Juanita always let the dog out whenever Kimba barked to go out, but they had a fenced backyard. She wondered if the dog had become infected at the groomers. The groomers handle many dogs each day, and some need to go out when nature calls. But she also thought that was highly improbable, for they are careful with animals in their care. Perhaps it happened when she walked her dog around the neighbourhood every day. Too often, many dog walkers do not pick up what their dog deposits on the ground. So, she accepted the tragic outcome in anger and frustration.

Immediately, Juanita longed for another dog to replace Kimba but realized replacing Kimba would be difficult. The family purchased Kimba from a reliable breeder. The dog had registration papers to prove her lineage as a pure breed. But things were different now with the onset of a full-blown pandemic.

Since the start of Covid-19, dogs had become in great demand, and breeders took advantage of this windfall by tripling their dogs' price. The price gouge did not sit well with Don, and he refused to pay $6,000 for a six-week-old puppy.

Don and Juanita loved animals and were fascinated by them. A friend suggested they adopt a dog from the Humane Society. The following day, Don called the Humane Society at Hopeville, where he lived, and in Dreamy Cove, a nearby city, to see if dogs were available for adoption. The managers at both locations thanked them for considering adoption, assuring Don that adopted pets are wonderful. Most had a loving home once, but illness or death inadvertently created circumstances whereby owners could not care for them anymore. Occasionally, a stray dog left to fend for itself craves loving care and is receptive to a human's love. A dog's unconditional love made such an impact in this couple's lives; they could not imagine living without one.

So, Don explained what happened to his dog Kimba and how Juanita, his wife, became saddened by the loss. Lana, the manager from the Humane Society at Hopeville, told Don that a male German Shepherd dog named Bruno was waiting patiently for someone to adopt him. Don told Lana he would bring his wife, Juanita, to come and look at the dog. Sara, the lady in Dream Cove, had only cats. However, Don would hear from her as soon as a dog for adoption became available.

At Juanita and Don's arrival, Lana led them to the kennel to look at the dog. It was an enormous brownish and black dog that had come in from the farm. The farmer who owned the dog sold the land and purchased a condominium in the city. The condo rules did not allow members with pets. Since the purchaser of the farm did not want the dog, he brought the dog here. When they came close to the dog, it wagged its tail in a friendly greeting. When they looked into Bruno's eyes, they were sad and forlorn. They seemed to beckon them to take him with them. Both Don and Juanita desperately wanted another pet, so they agreed to return the following day and take Bruno home.

On their way home, Don and Juanita kept saying how lucky they were to find another dog to replace Kimba. They continued calling him Bruno, the name given by the previous owner. Bruno translates to the colour *brown*. More commonly, German Shepherds' coats are a lovely mix of warm brown and black hues. But he might serve as a good watchdog and protect their home in their absence. With the decision made, tomorrow morning, they would bring Bruno home! But life does not always go according to plan. Occasionally, life plunks a detour sign in our path, and we find ourselves on a different road to our destination.

When Don and Juanita retired for the night, Juanita fell into a deep and restful sleep. When it was nearly time to awaken, Kimba appeared in Juanita's dream and filled her with great joy. Then something odd happened. Kimba talked to Juanita in the English tongue without a foreign accent. Kimba told Juanita not to bring Bruno home. She explained that Bruno's size and character were unsuitable for city dwellings. Bruno was a farm dog who loved to roam around the vast expanse of the farm and not cooped up in the fenced backyard of the city. His size would take up considerable space in their tiny house. When visitors arrived, the family would need to watch Bruno if he became highly protective of them. Kimba insisted they forgo bringing Bruno home and assured Juanita an ideal dog would be theirs in just one week. Then, as suddenly as Kimba appeared, just as suddenly, she vanished forever.

When Juanita awoke from her dream, she wondered what it all meant. She wanted to bring Bruno home, but Kimba advised her to wait just one week, and she would have the breed of dog suitable for them and appropriate for their pet. Juanita questioned herself. If she waited for a week and nothing happened, would Bruno still be available? How much credibility could one put in a dream?

When Don awoke, Juanita related her dream to him to determine his response. Don recalled an interesting comment made by Anatole France, a French novelist and journalist, who said, "To accomplish great things, we must not only act but also dream; not only plan but also believe." (*Works of Anatole France*) Don's suggestion was to wait and see. Kimba's idea made a lot of sense regarding the happiness of owner and pet. So, Don called Lana and told her they needed a week to think about adopting Bruno. Lana reminded Don she would not hold Bruno for them if another family came to adopt him.

Don and Juanita began the wait. Soon, three days went by with no results. Two more days went by, still no results. The couple wondered if they should have put any faith in Kimba. Would people ridicule them for listening to a talking dog in a dream? Still, they were adamant about carrying this dream to the finish line.

On the seventh day, Sara called from Dreamy Cove. She asked them if they were still interested in adopting a small dog as one became available that morning. An elderly lady who owned a toy poodle died of natural causes and left the dog to her daughter. Her daughter did not have the time to look after the dog because her job required much travel. So, she brought it in for adoption. If Don was still interested in adopting this animal, he could pick it up in the afternoon. The excellent news brought happiness back into their lives, and they rejoiced for waiting a week as Kimba had advised them.

The couple drove to Dreamy Cove, sixty kilometres from Hopeville, and Sara met them at the door. She told them that the owner named the female toy poodle Biscotti. The owner's daughter said the dog had a spirit that seemed to live on and on. This poodle demanded the owner's time and energy, and she was always up for a game of any kind. The information almost described Kimba. Without further hesitation, the couple agreed to adopt the toy poodle. Sara was happy to find someone so quickly to adopt the dog, and the couple was elated too.

But the dream made it so! Before they left for Dreamy Cove, Don brought out Kimba's food and water dish from the cupboard and placed them in the exact spot where they kept Kimba's bowl. On arrival home, as soon as they brought Biscotti into the house and released her, she immediately dashed directly to Kimba's water dish and began to drink. Juanita and her toy poodle bonded quickly, and soon the rhythm of their home became a new normal.

Bruno, the German Shepherd, was adopted by a family from a rural area near the city. He had the luxury of space in the country where he could run at will. It was a win, win situation for everyone.

The earliest recorded dreams began five thousand years ago on clay tablets in Mesopotamia. The Roman and Greek believed the Gods or dead relatives sent them messages and predicted the future. In 1899, Freud developed a psychological technique for interpreting dreams. In 1900, Freud believed that dreams manifested our deepest anxieties and desires. Donald and Juanita used their method; they listened to their dream and found happiness.

LESSONS

The Virtue of Patience

The greater that impatience grows, the quicker stupidity follows. Leonard was a middle-aged man who grew up in an egotistic society where speed became an everyday norm. But, along with a "me and now" community came an impatient culture. After a few mishaps from irrational moves, Lenny discovered that patience was a virtue cultivated through selflessness and the production of wisdom. The transformation happened slowly.

Leonard had a penchant for fast cars. One day, he walked into a Dodge/Plymouth automobile dealership, searching for a newer car and a speedier model. His old one had seen better days and was ready for the trash heap. When Len entered the premises, he was approached and offered assistance by an enthusiastic salesman who carried himself vigorously and gracefully. The salesman listened to Lenny explaining his need for a new vehicle that showed speed and power. The agent told Lenny he had two such used cars on the lot. The vehicles were both 1989 Plymouth Fury models with a V8 motor and a rear-wheel drive. One was red and the other blue. The company had discontinued making this model that year.

When the agent mentioned that the nameplate "fury" is Latin for "rage, extreme anger, strength or violence in action," the description convinced Len that the model matched his character perfectly. He checked with the salesman and determined the price of the red Fury. The salesman mentioned there would be a sale on used cars next month, but that bit of information seemed to have gone over his head. Whatever the price, he would pay it, but he must have the vehicle now. Therefore, he never squirmed over the price or suggested a lesser amount. Lenny made the down payment and signed the documents, promising to make monthly payments for the balance. He then drove the car home.

A month later, as he passed the dealership, he noticed the blue Fury on the lot with the price reduced substantially. Len felt like kicking himself for not waiting four more weeks. He had found it difficult to wait until the day of the sale. He would discover later that many things in life required patience to achieve a purpose without unnecessary expenses.

One morning, upset from an abrupt awakening, Lenny stared blankly into open space, propped himself up on his pillow, and pondered his next move. It was 5 a.m. and much too early for his morning ablutions. The sun's rays shone from the east through the bedroom window and bathed the hardwood floor with dazzling light. The family dog basked languidly in its rays as it lay sprawled on the bed, continuing to snore.

Lenny awoke at this early hour because a neighbour's car with a Hollywood muffler roared by his window. A Hollywood muffler is a glasspack, not very effective at silencing noise. Revving his motor as he passed by Len's window, the owner of a black sports car raced to work every morning for the past week with a noise that could awaken the dead. Presumably, he thought that everyone else should do likewise if he must rise so early. It amazed Len that no one complained of the noise to this early riser or the by-law officer. Lenny felt the time arrived to end this racket, for it had persecuted him for too long! He dispensed with the pleasantries and met fire with fire by bringing out the heavy artillery.

Len grabbed the clothes he wore the day before, dressed, jumped into his blazing red Plymouth Fury, slammed the door shut, and twisted the key in the ignition. Suddenly, 328 horses jumped at his command. He jammed the gear shift down and plunged the accelerator to the floor. The car's front end lifted several centimetres as he released the clutch. The Fury lunged ahead with accelerating speed. Smoke from the burning rubber, the exhaust fumes, and the dust mushroomed into the air as the car disappeared into the early summer morning air. When the dust cleared, two black tire marks were visible on the pavement by the officers in the patrol car behind him.

As Lenny approached the intersection, the green light turned to amber. Len thought the vehicle in front would proceed through the intersection on an amber light; it did not. It stopped as the light turned amber. He hurried to catch the neighbour, but following too closely, the noise of screeching tires shattered the air as rubber abraded the pavement, followed by a loud crash. Several minutes later, an ambulance siren pierced the morning air. The ambulance transported the occupant from the front car to the local hospital. Because Lenny saw the accident coming, he braced himself for the crash and suffered no injuries. Immediately, his anger abated when the police officer who saw the accident gave him a ticket for speeding and following too closely.

The following day, Lenny asked some of his neighbours if they had any complaints about the noise of the sports car at 5 a.m. each morning. Most neighbours had air conditioning units, and their windows were closed at night. Lenny had no air conditioning unit, so he kept his windows open at night, and heard all the traffic noise.

His impatience caused him to act spontaneously, resulting in a traffic violation and injury to a community member. He did not know that patience builds one's ability to be compassionate. Len needed to forget about personal desires and realize patience is a virtue during critical times. "Once bitten, twice shy" is an adage that has evaded him to date. In one instance, he lost money on a car purchase, and in another, he received a citation for a traffic accident. But there was more!

Just before Christmas, Len was flying home from a company sales trip. Soon after he arrived at the terminal, a winter storm raged. All highways were closed, and warnings were issued through the media to avoid all travel until the roads opened. The weather frustrated Len because he had many kilometres to go, and he did not wish to be alone in the city. His wife and family were waiting for him.

Rather than renting a motel room until the storm subsided, he got into his Fury and proceeded along the back roads to avoid the barricades. As he moved along the unbarricaded gravelled roads, the snow piling up made travel more difficult. Since no one travelled down this road from the storm's onset, the ditch alongside the road had filled up and veiled the road. Len estimated the centre road's location and cautiously proceeded to the junction. As he turned the corner that would take him to the main highway two kilometres away, the right wheels strayed into the ditch and hung up the vehicle. Len regretted his decision and should have remained in the city until the storm passed. Now, he must plan his next move.

Near the junction of the main highway and the gravelled road lived a farming family. Perhaps they would have a sofa he could sleep on while he waited for the storm to abate, he wondered. Or, they might have a tractor to pull him out of the ditch. So, Len got out of the car, slammed the door shut, and plodded through the snow on a two-kilometre hike to the nearest farmhouse. He hoped and prayed the family would be brave enough to open the door for him. He heard through the media that a child molester was released from prison in this area recently and could re-offend. So, people were now on high alert to strangers.

When Lenny arrived at the farmhouse, it was near 6 p.m. He knocked on the door, but there was no answer. Len tapped louder a second time, and from within came a sound of movement. The door suddenly opened, and a tall giant of a man calling himself Cameron asked Len why he was out in a storm on such a windy day. Lenny explained his desire to be home in Snorseville but needed to take the side road to avoid the barricade on the main highway. He acknowledged that his rash behaviour resulted in him becoming stuck in a snowdrift on the side road. Cameron felt sorry for Len's predicament and asked him to come in and join him and his family for supper. After supper, Cameron would take his tractor and pull the Fury out of the gully.

After a fine supper of fried chicken and baked potatoes, Cameron put on his Ski-Doo suit, winter boots and heavy mitts. He started up his John Deere tractor in the implement shed, asked Len to climb into the cab, and drove cautiously to the stranded Fury. After hooking the chain to the car, the tractor eased the Fury from its snowy restraint. Although Cameron refused payment for the tow, Len shoved a twenty-dollar bill into his snowsuit pocket.

Thankfully, the tractor made visible tracks for Len to follow to the main highway. It was easier going after that, for the storm was centred more to the south and less to the north near Snoresville. As Leonard's stress level slowly ebbed, he realized that sometimes things were not immediately clear. Impatience can cause you to make poor decisions, negatively affecting your health and happiness. Only through patient and perseverance do we discover the outcome. The selflessness concept became more apparent when Leonard faced the payback.

Lenny's company went bankrupt in the following year, and he became unemployed for several months. His employment insurance offered him a small income for several months, provided he searched for employment. Lenny kept going to the employment office daily to look for work but returned disappointed by the end of the day. After missing payments on his Fury, he received letters from the finance company that his car payment was overdue. The second letter warned him of his past due amount and possible vehicle repossession if he missed the next payment.

Unable to find employment, the thought of losing his beloved car worried him if he did not make a payment on his car. He hoped and prayed the finance company would be a little more patient with him until he found employment. When he begged and pleaded with the manager to give him more time, he found no compassion nor patience existed with them. He loved his car and did not want to lose it. He was at his wits' end!

Brent, one of Len's friends in a similar predicament, instructed Len to meet with a licensed insolvency trustee to discuss his financial circumstances. Brent's advice was a blessing. Len could sign a short, formal, legally binding agreement between him and his creditors that outlined how he would pay all or part of his debt at a reduced rate over a specified period, up to a maximum of five years. He could make regular, affordable payments based on his income and the size of the debt.

The trustee reviewed Len's financial situation, discussed his relief options, and advised him of the best path forward. The finance company relented and allowed Len to keep his automobile with those arrangements.

The patience concept finally made sense to Leonard. Self-absorption and compassion are contradictory terms. Only the former can exist in an egotistic society. However, suppose you want people to respect you for your compassion, patience, and concern for others; you must earn it.

Facing Daily Challenges

To succeed in life, you must have faith in yourself, not only in good times but also in times of challenge and criticism. When life hands you adversity that leads to stress, try to divert your energy into keeping yourself busy by doing something positive.

Matthew, like all humans, faced unique challenges each day. Climate change, world hunger, racism and war are among the global challenges we read or hear about daily in the media. These 'global challenges' require a global solution. But besides the global challenges, we still face personal challenges.

One day, Mathew felt a nagging pain in his stomach that would not go away. When weighing himself each morning before taking a shower, he noticed his weight going down by two kilograms each week. Matthew could understand the cause of the weight loss because of a lack of appetite and energy. Matthew disliked doctor appointments primarily because he feared hearing any bad results. But when he developed stomach pains and persistent vomiting, he made an appointment with his physician to have it checked out.

After a thorough examination and routine lab work, the doctor diagnosed Mathew with liver cancer and admitted him to the local hospital. The doctor's diagnosis presented the patient with two problems. The illness brought up a concern not only for his recovery but also his ability to get to the hospital. It was not because he could not walk but because the anti-vaxxers were protesting in front of the hospital and blocking its entrance.

In many cities, protesters were stationed outside hospitals, carrying signs, shouting at patients and health-care workers, and angrily expressing their opposition to mandatory Covid-19 vaccination policies. These protestors rallied outside acute care centres and interfered with patients and staff entering hospitals.

Matthew faced the admission challenge by having a police officer escort him to the hospital and enter the building with him. When conquering the first problem, he met the second and more serious medical challenge. Fortunately, the doctor discovered Matthew's tumour early, and the surgeon removed it in time. Matthew faced his challenge head-on and overcame the obstacles in his path. He believed in himself and pushed forward to overcome those challenges. Matthew became a long-term survivor when the doctor released him from the hospital.

Challenges in life bypass no one. The secret is to use them to one's advantage. Each challenge is an opportunity for personal growth and self-improvement. Ultimately, the goal is to use what you learn to grow and become the best you can be. If you mope and rebel against adversity, it will prevent any personal development. If you face it head-on, it will allow you to learn from those challenges and become a better person from experience.

It is much like learning to ride a bicycle. The moment you get on a bike, you can handle it with ease. At first, you may fall several times when you try. According to the adage, if at first you don't succeed, try and try again. Eventually, when you grasp the concept without mishaps, that ability stays with you for many years, even if the opportunity to ride a bike does not present itself for decades.

Sometimes, if taken, a well-intentioned professional's advice can also present a challenge. Then what do you do? Sally had a small Pekingese puppy, and she named it Scooter. She adored the little tyke! When they bonded, the dog followed her wherever she went. The problem arose when the veterinarian placed the dog on a special diet because of digestive issues.

The dog's stool was loose, and every time it defecated, its coat became soiled and needed a bath. The daily baths irritated Sally and presented her with an enormous challenge. The dog refused to eat the food the doctor prescribed, and Scooter had no energy. It slept most of the day and throughout the night. The doctor prescribed dry food to cure its diarrhea, but the dog refused to eat it. So, rather than selling the dog, she purchased some soft canned food at the grocery store, mixed in some leftover chicken from the dinner table, and added boiled vegetables to the mix.

When she placed the food on the floor, the dog wolfed it down and emptied the dish in one minute. When the dog went to relieve itself a few hours later, the stool was firm, and its coat was clean. From then on, Sally had no problems with soiled coats. She met the challenge and solved the problem.

In such frustrating situations, it's essential to look at the problem realistically. Sally realized that if she denied the reality of the problem, it would prevent her from finding a way of dealing with it. Washing the dog's coat every time it went out to relieve itself was not an option for her.

Occasionally, life puts us in situations that make us feel inadequate to meet the challenge. That is because, as mere humans, we can only do so much. We may have to face such complex problems that we cannot solve them with our best wisdom. Basil found himself in a similar situation one day. All his own efforts to save his life were in vain; he needed help.

During the Covid-19 pandemic, many people were infected with the Coronavirus and had difficulty breathing. Those infected were immediately admitted to the hospital and placed into an individual care unit. The seriously ill were placed on a respirator to help with their breathing. The occupancy of the ICU doubled and tripled as more infected patients were admitted. Soon the patients infected with Coronavirus filled the ICU and left no room for patients who required life-saving surgery.

However, the hospital cancelled all surgeries, and Basil must wait until the ICU reopened for patients who required an operation. Basil found himself between a rock and a hard place. His situation looked hopeless. He was desperate and worried that all the resources he could muster would not be enough. Loss is one of the biggest challenges we face in life.

Here Basil faced a problem too big for him to handle by himself. But Basil had good neighbours who offered him the help he needed, leading up to his surgery and throughout his recovery. Had Basil grown angry and resentful with the challenge life gave him, his bitterness would have stripped him of the joys of life during the three months prior to the operation. When Basil recovered from his illness, he was glad to have harboured no bitterness in his heart, only peace and tranquillity.

Occasionally, a challenge may come to those who make bad choices in life. When the sailing is smooth, the stress level is low. But, when a person marches to the beat of a different drum, the sea becomes choppy.

Gail graduated from university with an Arts degree and served as a stewardess on an airline. During the Covid-19 pandemic, the entire country feared the Coronavirus and rushed to the vaccination sites for the jab. Eventually, three-quarters of the country received two doses of the recommended vaccine. However, a third of the land became anti-vaxxers and refused to accept the vaccine. The anti-vaxxers argued that the government had no right to dictate what they should do or put into their bodies. Gail fell for the hype and chose not to receive a vaccination shot. She fell into the pro-choice category of supporters. Whenever she had a few days at home, she would join the protesters on the street near the hospital, wielding her anti-vaxxer or pro-choice signs.

One day, Gail came down with a severe cold after protesting on the street without wearing a mask. The covid test showed she contracted the Coronavirus and required treatment at the hospital ICU. At first, Gail downplayed her symptoms and claimed it was nothing serious, just a common cold. When breathing became difficult and she required hospitalization, she regretted her stance on vaccination. After much suffering, Gail died at the hospital with no underlying health conditions.

The side she chose in the controversy presented her with an insurmountable challenge. Yes, Gail willingly did what she wanted, and the price she paid was exorbitant! She paid with her life, and perhaps, the loss of many other lives she may have infected to fulfill her ideological stance. She could have changed her position on the ideology when scientists presented her with the facts. Changing her mind was her prerogative and her right. Deciding where you stand is an individual's responsibility. Tragedies are preventable in life through common sense.

Facing and overcoming complex challenges is a stimulating experience that can bring out the best in us. But this is true only if we have tools or skills suitable for the challenge. When a light bulb burns out in your garage, you buy a new one, climb a ladder, unscrew the burned-out bulb and replace it with a new one. Thus, you have saved time and money by doing it yourself and retained your self-esteem. But there comes a time in a person's life when the skills or tools are unavailable to meet the challenge. When we find ourselves in such situations, we must seek divine help. Joan found herself in a similar situation one day.

Joan was a wife and a mother. She had moved from Manchester to Canada after graduating from college in London. After several years in the nursing profession, she had married a gentleman who was well established in the legal profession. The couple now had three young children, so Joan chose to be a homemaker and look after their children rather than using a daycare service.

One day, she received a phone call from her parents in Manchester asking her to come to England for a few days while her mother recovered from major surgery. So, Joan hopped on the next flight to England and was in Nottingham within six hours. From there it was one hundred and thirty kilometres or two hours by car to Manchester. Her father picked her up and drove her home.

Joan helped with the domestic work for one week while her mother recuperated from her surgery. Joan packed her bag and booked a plane back to Canada when her mother was back on her feet again.

As the plane headed across the ocean to Canada, the aircraft experienced turbulence midway through the flight. Through the loudspeaker came the order to tighten their seats because the plane was in trouble. One engine had failed, and they may be going down for a crash landing. Joan was hysterical.

She got angry with God and said, "How could you do this? Three children and a husband need me! Dear Lord, restore the engine of this plane so I can get back home to my husband and children."

A couple of minutes passed, and the turbulence ceased. The announcement on the speaker told the passengers the engine was functioning again. With a sigh of relief, Joan thanked God for the miracle. The challenge Joan faced, she could not handle alone. But, if we pray, God will come to our rescue when He is desperately needed.

We meet daily challenges in sports, politics, religion and practically every walk of life. Life has its ups and downs. You can embrace it and enjoy the ride, joyfully learning from your experiences along the way, or you can become bitter and struggle through despair and depression.

The Value of Sharing

Many people think that hoarding money is the key to independence. Little do they realize that financial autonomy is impossible without financial knowledge and common sense. It's like a ten-year-old boy taking his father's car on a joy ride in the city. Soon, his joy ride turns into disaster as he hits a streetlamp and wrecks dad's car. To get to your destination safely, you must learn how to drive and watch where you are going. Keep an eye on the drivers ahead who may be signalling to turn or stop. Without basic knowledge and common sense, safe arrival at your destination rarely occurs. Similarly, these factors apply to the financial independence intended to necessitate life. If we look at the stages of human life, the concept of hoarding becomes more apparent.

It is interesting to note that humans pass through life in several stages. As we look back with affection at our childhood days, we marvel at the lack of stress and anxiety at that age. Babies live for the moment, caring only about themselves. They cry when they are hungry and expect their mother will feed them. When diapers are soiled, they wail and wait for mom to change them.

As kids, they spend many hours playing with their siblings in the backyard, oblivious to the cares of the world. Easter bunnies, tooth fairies and Santa Clause energize their thoughts; worries, fears, and responsibilities elude them.

These same selfish characteristics continue into their teen years but with vanity added to the mix.

Teenagers process much of their knowledge and experiences during their formative years. Through physical and hormonal changes, teenagers develop into adults. They find fault with their parents' viewpoints and rebel against their authority. When pride and vanity take hold of their lives, they view their parents as old-fashioned and uncool. Their life revolves around a self-perceived world and overlook their rebellious nature and its consequences.

Passing into adulthood, many carry their self-concerned behaviours, pride, and vanity from childhood. Adults soon concern themselves with praise, money, and their career. All these factors become so self-seeking that they overlook how time passes them, and they are getting older. All these factors play a prominent role in accumulating money and resources to the point of hoarding.

Unlike hoarding, sharing finds its genesis in social outings. When children get together, they form a bond of friendship and concern for others. Parents enhance these social skills by serving as models in sharing with neighbours and friends. A lack of these skills promotes hoarding. Research shows that "Widespread economic insecurities have cultivated a strong 'saving' culture among families. All these factors impact the identification, perception, and treatment-seeking of hoarding disorder." (Pathways)

How does hoarding differ from saving? There is a vast difference between saving for a rainy day and hoarding. A hoarder feels that whatever amount of money they have is not enough. They do not trust banks and worry that they will go broke and lose all their money. The likelihood of going broke is imminent and frightening to them. You are hoarding when you bury your money in a container in the ground. Eventually, if the hoarder dies before letting anyone know where he buried the money, it remains in the environment for many years until someone unexpectedly finds it. With savings, the average person knows that a certain amount of money is set aside for a specific purpose—investing for the future by putting it in a bank and allowing it to grow.

Money hoarders live a frugal life. These people deny themselves the luxuries of life and settle only for the bare necessities. When making a purchase, they hesitate and wonder if they should buy it. When something breaks down, they try to repair it themselves without the skills needed to succeed. They will take on two jobs, thinking this will provide them with more security. Jack fit the description perfectly.

Jack, a bachelor farmer, lived in a small bungalow his father built. When his father purchased the land, there stood an old, rat-infested shack on the property. The property had tall trees growing at the far end of the quarter section. His father chopped down those trees and used them to construct a log house for their living accommodations. With much labour and sweat, he completed the building before the snow fell. Clay and straw formed a paste to fill the cracks between the logs, preventing the snow and wind from entering. The completed building served as their home for many years.

When his father died, the land became Jack's property, as Jack was the sole survivor in the family. So, Jack became the owner and manager of the farming business. This sudden responsibility was daunting for him. He wanted to succeed in the industry but lacked the knowledge to achieve success. Regardless, he kept at it by following in his father's footsteps, and soon money flowed.

Jack deposited his hard-earned cash into the bank until he discovered that someone withdrew from his account without his permission. He complained to the manager, who assured Jack he would get to the bottom of this transaction. The following day, the manager informed Jack that one of the bank clerks withdrew that amount from his account as she did from a few other accounts to pay her gambling debt. The manager immediately fired her.

From that experience, Jack no longer deposited money in the bank. He emptied a litre jar containing cabbage soup for supper that evening, took the money he withdrew from the bank, and placed it in the container. Jack then screwed the lid back on it. Late that night, under cover of darkness, he dug a hole in an inconspicuous location and buried the money safely in the ground. Henceforth, this became his financial institution.

Jack continually worried he would not have enough money for his retirement, so he took on another job as a night watchman in the nearby town to supplement his income. To save more money, he lived frugally, buying only the bare necessities he required to survive. When something needed repairs, he tried fixing it himself even if he lacked the proper knowledge or tools to succeed.

Jack eventually became a recluse caught in the web of his own weaving. He drew the blinds in his house, and they remained drawn night and day. He would allow no one to enter his home. If a travelling salesman knocked at his door, Jack met him and spoke with him on the porch. It's not that he kept his house in shambles. His mistrust of people led him to believe everyone was out to get him and all he possessed. He became like a forgotten bead from a broken string.

When Jack turned sixty, he became ill and found himself in the hospital. Within two days after admission, Jack died. Since his money had remained hidden in a glass jar in an undisclosed location in the ground, funeral expenses remained unpaid until the sale of the farm. The money he buried in the ground remained there for many years. One day, when someone finds the stash, it will finally serve its intended purpose.

In stark contrast to Jack's life, there lived a man called Daniel. Dan lived in a small city with neighbours on both sides. He enjoyed life, had many social connections, and had a charitable heart. When a fire destroyed his neighbour's house one day, the family lost everything they had in the place. Dan came to the rescue and helped the family financially, and even gave them some of his clothes. He believed others would reciprocate his generosity if ever he required assistance at a critical time. Meanwhile, he found it rewarding to help those in need.

Many charitable organizations seek financial assistance for worthy causes. Dan turned none of them away without a donation. When a member of a charity organization came soliciting support for a particular need, Dan's chequebook came out, and a favourable gift put a smile on the solicitor's face. Several weeks later, the reward for his generosity came unexpectedly and in an unbelievable way.

Dan received an email advertising a lottery that a hospital had established to purchase an expensive surgical robot. It was one of the most expensive pieces of medical equipment used in health care, costing around $2 million per robot. Dan phoned the hospital and offered to purchase three lottery tickets at one hundred dollars per ticket.

Several months later, with all tickets sold, a draw determined the lottery winner. Much to his surprise and astonishment, they drew Dan's ticket. He became their one million dollar lottery ticket winner. It was true. Somewhere he read that when you give, you are more likely to get back a hundredfold. Dan put the money into his account and spent the remainder of the day in a state of controlled excitement. He thought about his winning and decided what to do with it.

Dan loved animals, and it irked him to see animals abused and starved. The next day, he made a trip to the animal shelter in the city where he lived. He recalled donating items to the Humane Society annual sale. The money helped defray the costs of accommodations and food for abused and homeless dogs. When Dan saw the need for a better and larger building for these animals, he donated part of his winning to subsidize constructing a modern animal shelter for the many dogs housed there. The money Dan contributed to the Humane Society provided a modern building to accommodate the animals crammed into the old building. Dan and the dogs slept well when the contractor completed the construction, knowing the shelter offered exemplary care for abandoned or unwanted dogs. Great exultation filled Dan's chest to the point of nearly bursting.

Researchers discovered that giving is good for your health. Stephen Post, a professor of preventive medicine at Stony Brook University, writes in his book, *Why Good Things Happen to Good People*, "Giving to others has shown to increase health benefits in people with chronic illness, including HIV and multiple sclerosis."

In a democratic society, citizens are responsible for their freedoms and should feel guilt for neglecting those responsibilities. Acquiring friends through giving and sharing tells the world you are kind and compassionate—a faithful Christian who helps those in need.

Dispersal of the World's Wealth

A loonie is of little worth, but it is an absolute treasure to a poor man. However, to an ethical person, the method of acquisition determines its actual value. Money is not harmful, but the greed that accompanies it is destructive. Money is one of the most convenient forms of barter. When gained fairly, used economically, and dispensed charitably, it can provide a decent standard of living to everyone.

The global Occupy Movement arrived in Montreal on October 15, 2011. University students raised an issue that questioned the inequitable distribution of wealth amongst the average and low-income earners. The founded Occupy Movement drew the world's attention to the lack of a fair and equitable dispersal of capital, with their slogan that 99 percent of the population holds only one percent of the money.

Economists observe that the gap between the rich and the poor seems to widen each year. Therefore, who is to blame for this unequal allocation of wealth—the dollar or society? From a loonie's perspective, it is highly opinionated on this distribution disparity and remains vocal on this issue, as you will note.

The first Canadian silver dollar was on the numismatic production line in 1935. It commemorated the Silver Jubilee of King George V. For fifty-two years, the silver dollar was in production, year after year, until the birth of the loonie. It was also a dollar coin, created at the Royal Canadian Mint in

1987. However, this coin is yellow-gold in colour and brass-clad in wrapping. "Loonie" was the nickname given to this new Canadian dollar, which derived its name from the loon (a Canadian waterfowl) on the reverse side. Being the first to come off the assembly line, he was the first to hear someone use the term "Handy Loonie."

Over the past quarter-century, Handy Loonie has had quite a remarkable life. It has been an exciting and colourful experience, as he fondly recalls. Always at the mercy of his many owners, used and abused at their discretion, this seemed to be his lot. Many twists and turns in the journey, replete with countless difficulties over the years; his entire life has been anything but mundane. Handy has graciously agreed to relate many of his quests and varied experiences before his retirement. From these diverse and colourful adventures, he can offer insight into the dilemma of inequality in distribution. The following is his rendition of some of his undertakings over the past twenty-five years:

Greetings and salutations, my dear capitalist friends! Handy Loonie is my name! Many prefer using the word 'Loonie' for short! The first part of the name, Handy, made its debut when I heard someone at a parking metre asking a friend, "Do you have a loonie handy for the metre?" Since then, the name has stuck!

Well, my life as a legal tender in the Canadian economy was an eye-opener. It began at the Royal Canadian Mint in 1987. I came out of a large sheet of brass-clad metal. At the start, a large machine, operated by the mint workers, punched a slug in the shape of a thin slice of summer sausage. When applied to both sides, the printing distinguished us from cheap silver nickels, dimes, and quarters that people often criticize for tearing holes in their pockets.

Those "silvers" always look arrogant and feign such superiority, presumably because of their popularity with parking metres and slot machines. But their snobbishness did not bother me. I had the advantage of size, and size always intimidates those of more diminutive stature. Being more massive, highly polished, and ornate gave me an edge. Stamped on the reverse side is a lovely loon, hence the name. The head of the Queen occupied the obverse. There was no way of knowing the extent of my popularity when placed into circulation! Ultimately, I would outshine all those snobbish silver coins despite my dark appearance. I have often heard derogatory remarks directed at the silver coins, calling them "change" or "chicken feed."

To my horror, I soon discovered some people would resort even to murder to possess the almighty dollar. Appreciatively, this world operates on wealth, power, and material possessions. It was a great feeling to know how desperate people were to acquire a buck. A need to belong is a powerful emotion. When achieved, it leads to one's well-being. However, at the onset, a dark complexion in a silver world provided dismal results in completing that quest. After its demise, many often longed for the renewal of the silver dollar's production. But belonging to someone was this heart's sincere desire, and colour would not be a deterrent.

Leaving the oily smell of machines in the Mint felt great! The workers squeezed twenty-five of us into a paper tube and placed us into a small canvas bag with other rolls of loonies and silver. Finally, they loaded us into a carrying case. I overheard two employees discussing the procedure of delivery to the bank. Two guards with pistols holstered at their sides carried us out to the armoured vehicle waiting at the Mint's entrance. Talk about royal treatment! Pondering on what great adventures were looming on the horizon, the future was full of anticipation and excitement.

The one-hour drive brought us to our destination. Once again, one of the armed guards picked up the carrying case and brought us to the bank along with the other guard by his side. The manager waited with bated breath for the shipment to arrive. My arrival would be the employees' first glance at a loonie just hot off the press. Would they express acceptance or rejection, I wondered? As they opened the end of the paper tube and slid us out, the entire staff got their first glimpse of a bona fide loonie. After a quick examination and several derogatory remarks about our colour, they placed us into a drawer with those haughty nickels, dimes, and quarters.

Beyond all the shiny silver, rolls of pennies lay segregated in the last section of the drawer. These coins were of a slightly different colour. Although much smaller than me, yet close enough to the hue, they warranted an introduction. It would have been interesting to strike up a conversation with them, but that never happened. The chasm between the loonie and the copper sections was too vast for a private chat.

Shortly after settling in, the drawer continued to slide open and shut repeatedly. At every opening, a stream of light would infiltrate the flat and interrupt our peaceful snooze. Often, only the silver would leave the drawer. On occasions, three or four rolls of silver vacated the drawer simultaneously. They were moving at such an alarming rate that it caused us to wonder whether our dark complexion caused their leaving. Only the coppers and loonies would soon remain sole occupants of the flat at this rate of departure. However, the following transaction put our worries to rest. The next time the drawer slid open, the clerk lifted several of us loonies out of bed and gave us to a customer who was the local grocer. With high expectations, we were now off to explore the world.

Arriving at the grocery store, a clerk loaded us in a coin dispenser at the end of the cashier counter. When the next customer paid for his groceries, I was ejected from the machine and shoved into the man's pocket. There were several nickels and dimes also resting there. As I was the largest of the bunch, it was easy to exert influence over them.

Several days later, the man left me at the diner as a gratuity for a young female server. She tossed me into the change pocket of her handbag among all the other feminine necessities occupying that space. The location was great! The scent of perfume was heavenly! Amongst all the paraphernalia lay a bright shiny copper. She introduced herself as Penny.

Penny seemed restless and depressed. She explained that copper is practically worthless today, only used as something to toss into a wishing well or maybe purchase a book of matches. Ugly rumours were going around those financial institutions about plans to do away with the copper family and unite it with silver. Economists reasoned those coppers no longer served their purpose in high finance and needed to go by way of the horse and buggy. She felt this was outrageous and outright genocide, and she was unhappy about it. Any attempt to cheer her up by philosophizing that electronics and plastic will soon replace all coinage proved fruitless. Then the unpredictable happened—mixed marriages.

To the surprise of many, through intermarriages, came the Toomey. It was made of aluminum, bronze and nickel. The progressive views by 1996 suggested the country was becoming open-minded about intermarriage. But it did not seem to improve Penny's disposition one iota, even though she approved of marriages between brass and silver. She drew the line when it involved a close relative.

The next day brought a new adventure. As the young server was rifling through her purse for makeup, she inadvertently let me slip out unnoticed to the sidewalk, and I hit the concrete with a ding. I surreptitiously rolled across the pavement and right into a window well of a building near the restaurant where she worked. The traffic noise drowned out the clink of my landing, making her unaware of her loss. I lay there for what seemed like a year before being discovered by a maintenance worker cleaning the window wells of debris. What a sigh of relief that produced! For many months, I envisioned this location becoming my permanent resting place.

The maintenance man then gave me to a beggar on the street. It was nearing the Christmas festive season. This poor, unkempt and unshaven soul was braving the cold weather for a handout. Along with a few of my brothers, he bought a hamburger and a coffee to quell his rumbling stomach. Everything beyond that is merely anticlimactic! My proudest moment arrived—feeding the oppressed and the hungry.

Continuing my journey, I passed through several more hands. Once, I served as a screwdriver, tightening screws for an electrician. I then lived through a harrowing experience as a moving target for a sharpshooter, who finally aborted his attempt after several misses. The next adventure was an encounter with a family who just struck it rich, winning a lottery. Their display of avarice I encountered was the epitome of human greed and self-centredness. It wasn't easy to understand why their windfall did not precipitate charitable results. Their poor relatives lived in poverty while the lottery winners hoarded their entire winnings.

The final journey to retirement began by accidentally stumbling into a hobby coin collector's hand at the car wash one day. The last person to wash his vehicle left several loonies on the coin receptacle and then forgot about them after the wash. Bill, a coin collector, noticed and picked up the money lying on the coin box and examined them. I was one of them. Now, at twenty-five, my coat was soiled and worn from excessive abuse and constant handling. The printing that identified age and denomination had eroded. These factors encouraged the collector to stop, take notice, and claim this find for his own.

Age and experience played an essential part in placing this quarter-century loonie in a special compartment of his wallet designated for coin keepers. He clad me in a cardboard jacket with a round window; inscribed beneath the jacket were these immortal words: 1987 rcm. This page became my final resting place, among many others, exclusively designated for future loonies. The time for retirement had finally arrived. It was heavenly! The binder became a mausoleum for silver, loonies, and pennies where kings, queens, and common loons rested together in peace and harmony.

Looking back over the many adventures experienced in the past quarter-century, I noted how people change when they suddenly come upon a windfall—a lottery win. It never is enough! A bottomless pit is impossible to fill. The more money people have, the more they want. Some will go to almost any extremes to acquire it. The irony is those who worry about not having enough money also worry about losing it when they finally have plenty. No one is happy with large bank accounts because they wonder what to do with the money before they die and must leave it to others. The thought of leaving it behind leads to more unhappiness and greed at its worst.

To collect all we need of this world by honest labour, to have wealth but not be controlled by it, is an ideal that human nature has a difficult time accepting. To that end, it is not the ones who have the most toys who win in this game of life, but those who have fun and play fair. How often do we see a hearse pulling a U-Haul to the cemetery?

As for the equitable distribution factor, many may feel that everyone receives their just deserts in this life. The more one puts into it, the more one gets out of it. It is a fact that our predecessors worked hard for their dollars. They put in a good day's work for the wages they received. They accumulated no vast fortune, but they were happy with their lot. Those who wait for handouts should take a lesson from their predecessors. Roll up your sleeves, get a job, any job, and work as they did. The fruits of their labour became evident in a few years. Self–esteem and progress evolved naturally from perseverance and hard work, not from grumbling and waiting for handouts.

I am glad to be out of this commercial arena and resting in peace. May the current production of loonies from the Royal Canadian Mint (rcm) enjoy the celebration of our twenty-fifth anniversary.

In recent months, the news media reported that some cities in Canada and the United States obtained a court injunction to remove Occupy Movement squatters off Crown land. With extreme reluctance, some left; others refused to leave voluntarily. Police physically removed those who refused to budge from the occupied sites.

Recently, further discontent among students provoked a march and a shutdown of the Jacques Cartier Bridge in Montreal. After twenty minutes, it reopened after police dispersed thousands of student protesters. However, discontent with the economic disparity between the rich and the poor continues to grow. A civil revolution, engineered by the young, is imminent if the gap does not narrow. That is my humble opinion!

The Music Man

God's gift of a free will opens the door to personal destiny. Occasionally, however, a mysteriously unexpected event in life offers a second choice. Despite the disappointment of attaining the initial goal, the second choice may be more beneficial, offer more perks, and bring more satisfaction than the first. A farm boy from the prairies first encountered this anomaly with trepidation but later accepted it with enthusiasm and zeal.

Richard spent most of his formative years in a farming community. Raymond and Brenda, Richard's parents, owned a half-section of farmland, which offered them a decent living. Farming was in Raymond's blood. He could not imagine earning a living any other way. He tried to instill the same passion for agriculture into his son. When Richard attended elementary school, Raymond would encourage his son to ride with him in the tractor cab while tilling the land. Richard loved working with his father and looked forward to each presented opportunity.

A one-room school stood nestled between two grain fields in the village nearby. The town boasted having seventy-five inhabitants. Parents transported their children to a city thirty-two kilometres away in previous years.

Several months before Richard's birth, Raymond had urged the community to construct a school in their community. Raymond had offered to donate three acres of land to the village for a school. Upon the school board's approval of accepting the tract, Raymond and ten other community members had formed a working bee and erected a one-room school. The school division supplied the desks and blackboards and hired one teacher for all eight grades. In September of that year, classes began, and Richard was born.

At six years of age, on his first day at school, Brenda brought Richard to the school his dad had helped build and introduced him to Miss Browne, his teacher. In favourable weather, Richard rode his bicycle one kilometre to school each day from then on. This practice was to be Richard's routine for eight years, and then he would need to be transported to the city nearby for the higher grades.

Richard enjoyed learning and discovering new ideas every day, but his love for the land remained foremost in his mind and heart.

When the snow melted in March, Richard would repeatedly ask his father, "When are you going to cultivate the field, dad?"

After Raymond cultivated the field in the spring, Richard, now a teenager, must harrow it. That is how devoted Richard was to the land. He was becoming a chip off the old block. Richard's enthusiasm for agriculture elated his father and never escaped his notice. Raymond felt secure in knowing that after his retirement, the entire half-section of land would fall to Richard. It was good to know the land would stay in the family for many years to come.

After graduating from grade eight, Richard occasionally pondered what more he could learn in the next four years of education. His mind felt completely saturated with knowledge; he wondered how many more hills lay before him to climb before reaching the top. Little did he realize that a mountain of expertise still awaited him as he scaled each upper grade.

High school classes were unavailable in Richard's community, causing parents to continue transporting their children to the nearest city thirty-two kilometres away. The school board purchased a bus and hired a driver for this purpose. Yet, an uneasy feeling persisted with the parents about that arrangement, for it offered them limited control over their children. The parents' concerns focused on the negative influence city students would have on their children, believing they would be led astray. Unlike other parents, Raymond believed his son stood on solid ground and anticipated he would not be disappointed in Richard. This feeling remained with Raymond and Brenda until their son entered Grade 12.

One day, Richard came home from school and told his parents that his school offered instrumental music to senior high students. One teacher, a church organist, agreed to impart her music knowledge to the seniors as part of the school curriculum. The only requirement was the necessity for students to purchase a recorder. She would first teach them theory in music and apply it to the practical aspects of a recorder.

Richard's love of music came from the radio his mother turned on every morning. The boy, intrigued by the prospect of playing an instrument, begged his parents to purchase a recorder for him. After some deliberation, Raymond agreed to drive into the city and buy the musical instrument for his son.

When his dad opened the package, Richard could not believe his eyes. He stared in disbelief at that twelve-inch wooden pipe. It had a mouthpiece at one end and a plug at the other end. On the tube, there were eight small holes someone had drilled into it. He wondered how this gadget could ever produce any semblance of music. In his mind, he imagined a recorder being something with strings like a fiddle or guitar. This empty wooden piece of pipe with holes in it made little sense to him! But he put it into his backpack and took it to school the next day.

When the bell signalled a change of classes, Richard walked into the music room with five girls and seven boys, all with recorders in hand. Each student chose a desk and sat down. Richard picked an empty desk near the front next to Sandra, the mayor's daughter from his village. He felt comfortable sitting next to her each day on the bus.

Then, Mrs. Jones, the church organist, walked into the room and introduced herself. She picked up her recorder and played a kindergarten ditty, "Mary Had a Little Lamb," for the class. Out of that twelve-inch empty pipe, his ears recognized the music to the song he had learned in the first grade. It was like magic! This miracle captivated him, so he couldn't wait for instructions to begin.

The music teacher was a kind and considerate lady who treated everyone as a novice. None of the students knew the rudiments of music. So, Mrs. Jones began with the basic theory. Attentively, everyone listened as she explained the notes on a scale and how to apply them to the recorder's holes. By November, everyone had grasped the theory aspect of music and was ready for the practical.

Mrs. Jones prepared a sheet of music with only the first three notes of the scale. She instructed the students to take them home, read the notes and practice them on the recorder. The assignment continued each week until students became familiar with all the notes and their location on the recorder.

The day soon came when all the students received a sheet of music for a familiar melody. At the baton's motion, everyone played the recorder to the tune of "Jingle Bells." It sounded astonishing to them! The students' progress impressed the instructor so much that she entered their musical item in the school Christmas concert just three weeks away. The students were super excited to display their musical ability to the entire community.

As the days rolled by, each student diligently practiced their piece, "Away in the Manger," during every spare moment they had. Every recess, they would give up their free time, meet in the music room, and practice. Within two weeks, they sounded professional and ready to display their talents to an audience.

One week before Christmas, all the parents received an invitation to the school's Christmas concert in the community hall. In the afternoon of that day, all the children rehearsed their parts before the show. After rehearsal, the teachers were confident the presentation would succeed with no mishaps.

At seven that evening, the hall filled up with parents and members of the community. When the concert began a half hour later, the principal went to the podium and welcomed the audience to the show. Before each presentation, the principal introduced the participants to the audience and explained the nature of their performance.

Finally, it was time for Richard and his class to play "Away in the Manger" on the recorder. The students fell into position on the stage as determined at the rehearsal. At the motion of the conductor's wand, the music filled the air with such a mystical sound that it seemed as though the baby in the manger was amongst them. The audience suddenly became as quiet as a mouse. Not a cough nor a rustling of paper interrupted their performance. When the music stopped, the applause was tremendous. The audience's response intrigued and amazed Richard so much; he vowed to continue his pursuit of music to a higher level. His love for farming was foremost on his mind, but the music was not far behind.

Upon graduating from high school, his parents enrolled him in a music program at the university. They purchased an inexpensive violin for Richard, thinking he could eventually play polkas, waltzes, foxtrots, and other dance music common in their locality.

Richard spent much time familiarizing himself with the violin and the location of the notes on the strings. The practice was repetitive, but the progress he made continued to hold his interest. He knew mastering the basics was worthwhile. And they were!

Soon Richard was playing simple pieces for his parents at home. They kept encouraging him to play some familiar old-time country waltzes. He obtained some dance sheet music and joyfully entertained his parents. Still, this music did not seem to fulfill his inner desire. He was seeking pleasure in hearing and playing music that stirred the soul rather than tapped the foot. So, his instructor introduced him to classical music.

The music instructor gave Richard two of the world's most famous classical music melodies—Serenade No.13 for Strings in G Major, composed by Wolfgang Amadeus Mozart in 1787. Richard would spend six hours on the masterpiece and then switch to Beethoven's Symphony No.5 in C Minor. He became proficient at both masterpieces, but his parents were disappointed that Richard would not channel his talents to dance music. They enjoyed listening to him play those oldies.

The tunes gave them much pleasure and brought back fond memories.

Richard was in a log jam. He was spending too much time on classical music and neglecting his duties on the farm. He was also thinking of marriage but had dated no girls yet. Richard reached a critical point in his life, the necessity to make crucial decisions. He came upon a plan one evening that would solve all his problems.

The next day, Richard placed an ad in the city newspaper, looking for a female guitar player interested in forming a local band. He specified she must be able to sing and also willing to travel.

Within a week, Richard received a phone call from Autumn, an interested female musician who seemed to fill the requirements. She and her mother arrived at Richard's apartment, where he explained his desire to form an old-time musical dance band. He envisioned the band playing for weddings and socials in the city and rural communities. The mother and daughter expressed interest in the idea, and the daughter agreed to become part of the band. She also indicated that her sister and brother-in-law were thinking of forming a band. Her brother-in-law, Aaron, was a drummer, and her sister, Amber, was an accordion player. Richard asked Autumn to bring the couple along the next day to join his group. They would also give their band a name.

The following day, the four met and reviewed all the details of finances and travel, and then they named the band. They called themselves Icebergs because it displayed the tip of the band's capabilities. Their listeners would be left with much more to discover. Before everyone left, they agreed to meet at Autumn's place and practice old-time dances together.

After several practices, the band sounded ready for hire. Richard placed signs on billboards in rural communities around the city and an ad in the city newspaper. Soon a request came to play at a country wedding.

The members of the band worked well together and became popular with the people. Autumn's mellow voice appealed to the mature audience. Her talent brought popularity to the band, as well as many requests to play at socials. Her presence enamoured Richard, and one day, he found the courage to ask her out to dinner at a classy restaurant. She accepted the invitation. She had a very pleasing personality and a smile that lit up the room when she entered it. From then on, they dated regularly.

When Richard told his parents about the band and the girl he was dating, they were ecstatic. He also told them the music genre they were playing. His parents could hardly contain themselves to hear such fantastic news. Their hopes and dreams of having their son at home helping with the farm would now be a reality.

As for Richard, his preference was still classical music, but he found dance music uplifting. His greatest joy was watching the dance halls filled with people who appreciated his band's talents. It reminded him of a virus that infected the young and old alike. Richard's dream was to bring some appealing changes to the younger generation.

After dating Autumn for a year, Richard proposed marriage to her, and she accepted. After Richard and Autumn exchange their marriage vows, they built a house in the same city where Richard received his high school education. This location is where the band would maintain its office.

Gradually, the Icebergs changed the old-time genre and incorporated some current popular songs of their generation.

The Icebergs became a big hit and in great demand. Richard and Autumn were well pleased with their success.

How does Richard feel about these arrangements? Richard explains that when playing, he is in a world of his own. Richard feels away from his body, in another world next to his wife, who sings like an angel. The unexpected offered him an alternative way of life with many perks and great satisfaction. What more could he ask for?

Benevolent Deeds Eclipse Malign Influences

Somewhere between junior high and senior high, many teens decide on their vocation in life. Parents, teachers, and/or counsellors can offer some good advice. At other times, the individual chooses independently. Whatever the choice, it helps to glance back at the past, take a realistic look at the present, and then pick a future path. This method can become a helpful guide for choosing a vocation and a role in society.

Occasionally, some prefer the path of least resistance and become parasites who feed on others. These scammers prey on the vulnerable and defraud the hardworking, honest man. The benevolent will muster all their energy, effort, and abilities into developing their good character. They will become productive, worthy citizens of their community and society. Sadly, shady characters can influence some people's choices of vocations. These bad influences were impressed upon Johnny during his formative years. However, as maturity set in, so did his outlook.

Johnny lost his mother and brother in an automobile accident at six. His father soon remarried, and his stepmother became Johnny's mother after the mishap. His family lived in an urban community where the crime rate was high, and employment opportunities were scarce. The boy's small stature earned him the affectionate title of "Little Johnny." Both of Johnny's parents worked, leaving him to spend much of his free time alone. When boredom overwhelmed him, Johnny had difficulty staying out of trouble. Due to a lack of adequate parental support, authorities placed Johnny in a foster home.

For several years, his misdemeanours abated, but problems resurfaced when he hung out with the wrong group of boys. His deplorable behaviour caused him much grief as he struggled through his last year of elementary school. At first, his antics were trivial and a nuisance, but then he became a menace to society and a problem to his foster parents. Johnny often became involved in some mischief and received a reprimand from his guardians.

For example, one day, as he was sitting on his front step, he watched a neighbour's cat defecating on his lawn. The feline's presence inspired Johnny to teach the cat a lesson. He called the cat over and petted it for a while. Then he attached a string to an empty tin can, tied it to the cat's tail and released the animal. The feline became frightened by the rattling can and tore wildly about the yard as if possessed. Johnny busted a gut as he watched it in agitation.

On another occasion, he snuck into an unattended car idling in a driveway and took it for a joy ride to relieve his boredom. Luckily, a policeman in a cruiser spotted him behind the wheel and shortened Johnny's ecstatic experience.

At twelve, he hot-wired a neighbour's car and drove it at an excessive speed down a rural gravel road, narrowly avoiding a head-on collision with an oncoming truck at a sharp S curve. The shaken driver reported the incident to the local police.

Unremorseful, Johnny merely laughed when apprehended and replied, "It was fun! That's how I get my kicks!"

He knew that juveniles escaped severe reprisals from the law for all such misdemeanours.

At eighteen, still in Grade 10, the school became so unbearable, it caused him to abandon his studies and leave. Book-learning bored him. His mind was constantly dwelling on excitement and pleasure. He lived by the motto, "maximum pleasure with minimum effort." He followed that course until he reached his twenty-first birthday.

One day after his twenty-first birthday, Johnny sat alone on a park bench, reminiscing about the good old days. As he reflected upon the countless pleasures from his past experiences, he suddenly realized that his pursuit of "kicks," as he called it, had caused him much grief and many inconveniences to others. This surprising turn of mind astounded him that day. As he sat there all alone without a friend in the world, his heavy heart soaked in self-loathing and remorse. He felt like a jerk for causing all those problems to innocent victims in his community. He immensely regretted his grossly abhorrent behaviour. It no longer excited nor amused him, even just thinking about it.

It boggled his mind, and he wondered how he could have derived any enjoyment from such senseless actions. If he continued to move along this same course any longer, he reasoned, failure and incarceration were just a matter of time.

He understood the reason many slip into alcohol and drug addiction. This habit wasted many lives and paved the city streets with users. Johnny felt sorry for all those wretched homeless people in the city searching for a bed at night during a storm or begging for a hot cup of coffee in the morning. He shuddered to think this could also happen to him if he didn't alter his course. As he pondered these frightening thoughts, he was now more determined that "Little Johnny" would not rank among the many more that gave up trying.

Continuing to reminisce, Johnny recalled how he would hang around with some of the older boys he called friends. It made him feel more mature, associating with them as his role models. Johnny admired Snake for his carefree, irresponsible ways and his flagrant disregard for the law. Snake never mentioned his real name, but the other gang members poked fun of him and his fear of snakes.

It impressed Johnny to watch Snake confront the police, lipping off to the officers when they accosted him for jaywalking, and then flipping them off as they were leaving. Now Snake's character quickly diminished for Johnny, and the admiration of him dwindled. Eventually, Snake served time in jail for selling drugs. The number of lives he affected and destroyed by his actions was immeasurable.

Then there was his other friend, Giver. The nickname Giver stuck because whenever he was riding in someone's car and they were going too slowly for his liking, he would say to them, "Giver!"

Johnny recalled the evenings when he met Giver walking his dog along the avenue past Johnny's home. He wondered why Giver's daily walks were so irregular. One day, Johnny tailed him to a neighbour's residence. It seemed odd for Giver to suddenly slip inside a neighbour's house through the back door soon after the neighbour left for the golf course. Since no one locked their doors in this suburb during the day, Giver found it convenient to rob his neighbour without getting caught. The picture now became noticeably clear. Giver stole from occupants' homes while they were away. He was trying to support his drug habit by whatever means he could.

Then Johnny thought about Snooker, the kid on the dole. Johnny never did know his real name. The gang called him Snooker because he loved to play snooker, the daddy of all billiards games! If you needed to find him during the winter months, you could check one of the billiard tables nearby.

Snooker kept coming home every winter with the same excuse, complaining there was no work for him. Somehow, he held a job during the summer just long enough to become eligible for employment insurance benefits. By November of each year, his position seemed to vanish into thin air like the fog on a sunny morning. Everyone in the community knew that Snooker was lazy and hated to work. But the necessity of survival dictated a mediocre work ethic.

Flats was also quite a character. Whenever one of his gang members asked for a buck, he would always tell them he was flat broke. Hence his nickname, Flats!

Flats always complained that our government system was unfair because it helped the prosperous but neglected society's most impoverished. It never entered Flat's mind then that he had every opportunity to become a success in life. Had it not been for those frequent visits to the local pub, he would not have been in this predicament. He should have realized that the government was helping Flats regardless of his undeserving ways. He was on social assistance, receiving welfare benefits to which the working people contributed. Johnny removed him off his good-citizen list along with Snake, Giver, and Snooker.

Johnny was now more determined than ever to avoid ending up like his friends if he could help it. He would do his best to stay out of jail, complete his high school education, and find suitable employment to improve society. He would exclude his so-called friends as mentors. Nothing would deter him from becoming a good citizen of his community. In Johnny's opinion, many in his district stood out as perfect examples of good citizens.

He recalled some of the good citizens in his community. He found it difficult to hold back those feelings of remorse when remembering the time when he pushed a younger boy into the mud puddle at a construction site. The boy, a walking mudpack, appeared all soaking wet and dirty. His appearance was so comical that it caused Johnny to burst out laughing until his sides hurt. Just then, an older woman walking by came to the rescue, cleaned the dirt from the boy's face with some Kleenex, scolded Johnny, and walked the victimized boy home.

Johnny also recalled the constant lectures in his classroom and the many warnings about drugs and alcohol while driving. He remembered the offer his teacher made to assist anyone who became inebriated and required a ride home. Johnny was not impressed with do-gooders then. The good Samaritan act was not for him. It was a good topic for a Sunday sermon at church, but this was a dog-eat-dog world. It was everyone for himself!

As he compared the two groups of people, the "me, me" group and the "others first" group, he now wished to be part of the latter group. The importance of "helping others in times of trouble" was now his motto and goal.

In another benevolent incident, Johnny was changed after teasing the neighbour's dog. He loved to watch it bark and growl at him, but only from a safe distance. The dog, when tied to a stake in the yard, was unthreatening. On this day, when the teasing began, the Doberman became unchained. While being provoked, the dog bolted at the miscreant. When Johnny discovered it was unfettered, he panicked but was sure he could outrun that mangy mutt. However, the dog was much faster than he had anticipated. While maintaining his retreating speed, Johnny glanced back to determine the dog's location. He sweated when he noticed that it was closing in on him.

Then it happened. Crash! Johnny ran smack dab into Mr. Goodman. The man looked somewhat shaken at first and mumbled some vague unpleasantries under his breath. When the man finally got hold of himself, he chased the dog away. Johnny went home smarting after receiving a severe reprimand.

Then, nearing his twenty-first birthday, a neighbour of Johnny's was a Godsend to him. One evening, Johnny was itching for something to steal. He skulked over to the neighbour's garage, found a flashlight lying on the workbench, and pocketed it. A police cruiser spotted Johnny sneaking into Mr. Small's garage. They caught Johnny red-handed, stealing the torch and accosted him. Johnny explained that he was borrowing it from Mr. Small to find the pocketknife he lost in the alley. When they asked the owner to substantiate Johnny's defence claim, Mr. Small acknowledged that he permitted Johnny to take the flashlight. What a lucky break for him! Johnny was so thankful; he let out an audible sigh of relief.

The next day, he came and thanked Mr. Small for his act of kindness. After a brief lecture from Mr. Small, Johnny promised to change his selfish ways. He made right his promise.

As Johnny reflected upon the many other wrong moves, he suddenly felt a 180° turn inside him. His entire outlook on life changed. His old ways seemed so crude, senseless, and repulsive. Those old ways would disappear like the winter snow on a warm spring day. As his character transformed into a new charitable type, Johnny's new way seemed a lot easier for him to handle. Now his path stood clear and unobstructed.

Johnny returned to complete his education and received his high school diploma. Johnny's father and stepmother assisted him financially in his studies at the university level for three years. Johnny graduated with a bachelor's degree in sociology. The knowledge qualified him to obtain a position with the Canadian Child Welfare System. Johnny set an important goal to see that others got a second chance in life as he did. Little Johnny became a conscientious worker and a model citizen.

We should not assume that the bad outweighs the good in our society. It takes just a few good examples to create a positive impact on someone, helping them to choose a straight and narrow path in life. It took just a few Good Samaritans to tilt the scales toward choosing a decent and honest life. The few good examples outweighed the many bad ones by a hundredfold. Johnny was so grateful for all the kind people who were instrumental in redirecting his life in the right direction. These good people helped him avoid incarceration and set him straight on the road to becoming a productive citizen.

Many Facets of Power

Margaret Thatcher, a former prime minister of England, once said, "Power is like being a lady . . . if you have to tell people you are, you aren't." Her observations are accurate when we think about visible brute strength, like a volcano erupting and spewing lava high into the atmosphere or a tornado ripping off rooftops and splintering trees in its wake. But the faces of power come in many shapes and forms, some not as apparent to the naked eye—one such facet of power comes in love.

Love is such a powerful force binding a man and woman together for life. This abstract entity is not its hormonal factor and must be proven to warrant its existence. Is it true love when the consequence of such love is demanding and controlling? Does true love force one person's ideals on another? The core differences between two people may vary, even though they seem right for each other. The man who enjoys attending hockey and football matches differ from a lady who prefers opera and ballet. They must compromise to make their union work. Establishing an open line of communications to identify those differences and settle them will promote a lasting relationship. Focusing on the other person's needs without neglecting some of your own needs shows you love and care for your mate. Romantic and agape love must intertwine to bind and promote unity in marriage.

This letter written by an unknown person expresses a false example of love.

> *Dearest Jimmy,*
>
> *No words could ever express the great unhappiness I've felt since breaking our engagement. Please say you'll take me back. No one could ever take your place in my heart, so please forgive me. I love you; I love you; I love you!*
>
> *Yours forever,*
>
> *Marie*
>
> *P.S. And congratulations on winning the lottery.*

A further example of power lies in beauty. Beauty is present only in the eyes of the beholder. One person's view of a painting will affect the spirits of that observer immensely but will not affect another. The options of beauty are vast, and its interpretation is dependent on one's preferences. Although a beautiful painting gives the viewer an unreal feeling of life, it offers the beholder an improved experience of the world. In his book, *Nach Der Schule*, Winckelmann, a German art historian, claims beauty should possess three key factors: "The beauty of form, the beauty of an idea, and the beauty of expression," which, he says, "is only possible in the presence of the first two factors." A painting with its explosions of many sunburst colours may not be as appealing to those who prefer a more subtle expression of life as in Vincent van Gogh's "Early Workers" paintings.

The beauty of a woman offers a powerful image that turns most men's heads. Lingerie commercials prefer using beautiful models in their advertisements. Most men always give a beautiful blonde woman a second look. Sam Jarrett contributed this humorous article about beauty to *Reader's Digest*. "My wife was grading a science test at home that she had given to her elementary school class and was reading some of the results to me. The subject was 'The Human Body,' and the first question was: 'Name one of the major functions of the skin.' One child wrote: 'To keep people who look at you from throwing up.'"

Next to beauty is the peace that commands great power when established. But what is it? Is peace a nice quiet day spent with family at the cabin by the lake, or is it a day when the Taliban runs out of ammunition in Afghanistan? When listening to the news each day, a bombardment of information reveals we live in turbulent times. The Covid-19 pandemic exacerbated the situation further with the anti-vaxxers. How is it possible to keep one's sanity in such a world? Is peace even possible?

We all wish for peace in life's troubling times. Will passing time change the world for the better, or is that even possible? God is our only hope. To maintain serenity, we must proceed in a calm spirit. In Saint Francis de Sales' booklet entitled *Saints in Times of Crisis,* his advice is "Do not lose your inner peace for anything whatsoever, even if your whole world seems upset."

The power of peace can be a fickle master. In the comedy series *Two and a Half Men*, Charley, the uncle, always has the upper hand over his nephew Jake. One day, Charley inadvertently ran over a cat when backing out of his garage. Thinking it was his fiancée's cat, he feared telling her about it. Jake was there when the incident happened. Suddenly, Jake finally had something over Charley and disobeyed him with that knowledge. Jake threatened to tell Chelsie about the dead cat if Charley refused to let Jake drive his expensive BMW car. Here Jake was at peace, Charley in turmoil. But, when Chelsie came over for a visit with her live cat in her arms, suddenly Charley was peaceful; Jake was in turbulence for threatening to blackmail his uncle. When Charley discovered it was the neighbour's cat, and the neighbour was twice the physical size of Charley, Jake once more regained his power.

When President Biden withdrew his American troops from Afghanistan, suddenly, the power shifted to the Taliban. When their guns spoke, protesters disbanded, and traitors died. That brings us to the power of truth.

Truth is an abstract entity that defies full definition. Pilate first asked the question of Jesus, "What is truth?" nearly two thousand years ago, and the question remains unanswered to this day. We merely get partial revelations of it, somewhat like lightning flashing across the sky. Partial disclosure comes when clouds of negative and positive charges collide and discharge a spark, making it visible to the naked eye. Occasionally, flashes of lightning darting across the sky change to phases of sheet lightning hidden beneath the clouds that never reveal themselves fully. Likewise, we never get a complete and total definition of truth. If we say truth is "that which we believe," that is too narrow a definition.

For example, recently, someone exposed his belief that the earth is flat and if you travel far enough to its edge, you will fall off the planet. Yet, scientists discovered through experimentation that the world is round. Satellites circled the earth, sending pictures of the roundness of the earth. Truth means seeing things as they are and not as they are presumed to be. Perhaps the truth is so profound that the capacity of the human mind cannot grasp its magnitude.

Happiness is another facet of power to explore. "Happiness," a cynic once said, "can only be found in the H section of the dictionary." Happiness is another abstract entity that defies definition. It is a joyful emotion precipitated by contentment and fulfillment. These positive factors that satisfy life are influential, self-seeking factors to happiness. Ironically, this feeling comes with a full range of emotions. When the cup of happiness is full, somebody always comes along and jogs your elbow! When rain falls on your parade, a happy person occasionally becomes angry or sad.

The secret lies in a person's ability to handle difficulties in life without blame or bitterness. Such a person is always optimistic. They know things will get better and can manage the setbacks. In PubMed Central, research shows that happiness promotes better health, and these positive emotions extend the duration of life by a decade or more.

Nathaniel Hawthorne writes that "Happiness in this world, when it comes, comes incidentally. Make it the object of pursuit, and it leads us on a wild goose chase, and is never attained. Follow some other object, and very possibly, we may find that we have caught happiness without dreaming of it." (Brainy quotable quotes)

Randolph, a druggy, can readily relate to that comment. He was a drug addict who convinced himself happiness existed encapsulated in a pill. But obtaining such happiness was illegal and required vast amounts of money. To feed his habit, Randy chose the crime of home invasions. His escapades ended abruptly when a security camera caught him in the act and landed him in jail. While incarcerated, he overcame his habit and discovered the serenity of the

Bible. God's words became a proxy for drugs. Living out his sentence in jail led him to the true happiness he sought all his life by merely changing his character without deteriorating his health. The powerful words of prayer were his salvation.

When listening to someone giving a speech on a fascinating subject, you will notice the power of their words. Words are so powerful that they confirm our beliefs, direct our behaviour, and shape our world. For example, the energy of words manifests itself when someone in an attendance hall yells, "FIRE!" The audience screams, and the panic that follows becomes chaotic. Occasionally, people become trampled and injured during the evacuation. A touching sermon at a funeral evokes powerful emotional responses to the pastor's words. A heartrending romantic story brings tears to the reader's eyes. Those who constantly criticize others have a way of dragging their listeners down.

Dr. Masaru Emoto's experiment in testing the power of the spoken word surprised everyone. He placed a cup of cooked white rice in two mason jars and screwed on their lids. He labelled one jar "thank you" and the other "you fool." He placed both jars in an elementary school. Twice a day for a month, students spoke the words "thank you" to one jar and "you fool" to the other jar. On the last day of the experiment, when Emoto opened both jars, he found the rice in the insulted container shrivelled into a black gelatinous mass. The rice in the kindly treated vessel remained white and fluffy. Such is the power of words. Words in prayer are crucial in our relationship with God.

Faith is a powerful force! It encompasses all other virtues and leads to everlasting life. It overcomes obstacles that hinder the path to destiny. In his book *Faith*, G.K. Chesterton writes, "To love means loving the unlovable. To forgive means pardoning the unpardonable. Faith means believing the unbelievable. Hope means hoping when everything seems hopeless." Who could or would want to resist such a powerful force?

A man stands on the corner of two busy streets holding up a sign reading "Trust in Jesus." He is a street preacher whose faith in God is exemplary. A couple comes knocking at your door and offers to read the Bible to you. They are members of the Jehovah's Witnesses sect. They are there because the Bible says, "Whoever is ashamed of me and my words, the Son of Man will be ashamed of them when he comes in his glory and the glory of the Father and the holy angels." (Luke 9:26) Having a strong faith in Christ compels them to share God with others.

On SermonIllustrations.com, John Emmons explains faith in this manner: "The African impala can jump to a height of over ten feet and cover more than thirty feet. Yet, these magnificent creatures can be kept in an enclosure in any zoo with a three-foot wall. The animals will not jump if they cannot see where their feet will fall. Faith is the ability to trust what we cannot see, and with faith, we are freed from the flimsy enclosures of life that only fear allows to entrap us."

Faith is such an essential virtue, for it opens a person's eyes to the reality of life and overcomes fear and timidity. Through faith, all things are possible with God. Through prayer, God's love, peace, truth, and happiness will beautify our world as we face turbulent times. On SermonIllustrations.com, Martin Luther says, "God our Father has made all things depend on faith so that whoever has faith will have everything, and whoever does not have faith will have nothing."

STRUGGLES

Total Rejection

One quiet summer afternoon, Roberta was sitting on the deck at home, nursing a cup of coffee and catching up on the latest trends in *Chatelaine*. Suddenly, the phone rang and diverted her attention from an interesting article she was reading. The call came from a local adoption agency. In a calm and assuring demeanour, a government counsellor dropped a bombshell on her. He stated that her half-brother was looking for her. He assured her that this phone conversation was merely a preliminary method of inquiry. A letter would be forthcoming, subject to her approval, detailing information regarding this matter.

Most of us know that anything out of the ordinary breeds skepticism and suspicion. This call came as an enormous surprise to Roberta, creating confusion and distrust.

For sixty years, Roberta had known she had a brother, Adam, and a sister, Sylvia, who were considerably older than her. Roberta's guardians, Morris and May, led her to believe that she was their biological offspring and not Sylvia's unplanned child. As a single mother, Sylvia could not care for Roberta, so her mother agreed to adopt Roberta. Along with financial support, the father disappeared without a trace when he became aware of the pregnancy. The guardian's reluctance to be upfront with Roberta is understandable. Many parents find it dicey, responding to young children's questions about their origin. Adoptive parents worry about how best to answer the question: "Where did I come from?" However, councillors encourage parents to tell children as soon as possible that they are adopted rather than to hear it from other children. So, the notion that her half-brother was looking for her just came out of the blue.

Yet, Roberta wondered why Adam and Sylvia were so much older than her! Perhaps the age difference was an unwanted pregnancy, her birth! Roberta could imagine the surprised look on her mother's face when faced with an unwanted pregnancy. Yet, she never treated Roberta like an unwanted child or as an accident! Through her formative years, the short time spent with Adam and Sylvia created a strong bond of love, which formed her identity. Now, however, the phone call baffled her.

The nagging question now was, "Who is this half-brother that is searching for me?" Was Adam her half-brother? Adam lived in the city and knew that Roberta had taken residence in another province. He knew her address and phone number. Why did he not just pick up the phone and call? She wondered.

A week after the strange phone call, the expected letter arrived from the local adoption agency. It outlined the responsibility of the agency to connect mutually agreed upon adopted children with their siblings. Carl Smith was attempting to establish contact with his half-sister, Roberta, and requested a willingness to comply. Roberta opened the message with great trepidation.

Her initial reaction to the letter was to check the calendar to determine whether it was April Fool's Day. It was not! The next step was to call Sylvia and make inquiries about a possible relationship with Carl Smith. Her parents had long passed on, so Sylvia and Adam were her only contacts for information and clarification. What Roberta discovered during their conversation that day caused her to rethink her entire life.

Roberta's alleged sister Sylvia indicated that she was Roberta's biological mother but had given her up for adoption at birth to her own mother. Since Sylvia was not married during Roberta's birth, she could not independently take care of a child. This information almost blew Roberta's mind. So now, her sister was her biological mother, and her assumed mother was now her grandmother. What confusion!

Moreover, Carl was Sylvia's second child born out of wedlock to a different father, and therefore, he was Roberta's half-brother. The Smith family adopted Carl. Sylvia cautioned Roberta to keep this information strictly confidential. Sylvia's husband was not aware of this hidden segment of her single life.

Roberta mentioned to Sylvia that the adoption agency inquired whether she and Carl could meet one day. However, Sylvia cautioned Roberta not to contact Carl lest he try to locate his biological mother's address. Sylvia indicated that initially, Carl attempted contacting her, but she refused. She felt it was her prerogative to do so, she affirmed, and was not open to discussion! Carl's appearance on Sylvia's doorstep would make the situation uncomfortable and awkward to explain to her husband.

After a week of deliberation, Roberta decided to establish contact with Carl contrary to Sylvia's request. However, the meeting would initially be through the adoption agency. The counsellor's suggestion was to keep expectations of the relationship low and take things one step at a time. He reasoned that it is easy to get caught up in the moment and leap forward when emotions are high. He advised taking time to ease into the relationship and build a strong foundation in the first stages. The agency would send a letter to Carl, indicating that Roberta agreed to establish the contact he requested. When Carl received the agency's message, the onus would then be on him to initiate the connection, either by letter or phone. He phoned.

When Carl phoned, the initial conversation began somewhat strained, but as it progressed, a friendly atmosphere developed, and their conversation flowed freely. After several more calls, Carl was finally welcomed and accepted as her half-brother.

In one of their many dialogues during the year, Carl explained how he had tried to reach Sylvia, his birth mother, and how deeply hurt he was when she refused to acknowledge him. This rebuff so upset him that he was about to give up, knowing he would never get to meet his biological mother. Carl was at the point of tears because of her refusal. But upon pondering on this subject further, he thought of another avenue to explore. When he learned that he had a half-sister, perhaps she would provide him with pertinent information about his mother.

Carl's plan got overly complicated. Carl wanted his birth mother's address; Sylvia was adamant that Roberta not give him her address. Roberta found herself placed in a difficult situation.

Stewing over this problem was stressful. Disclosing Sylvia's address to Carl would create unpleasant consequences for Sylvia, her family, and Roberta. The thought of Sylvia ostracizing Roberta forever was not an attractive option. Yet, not disclosing Sylvia's address to Carl may discourage him from opening any further communication channels. That was also an undesirable consequence. As an alternative, the proposal was to send him a picture of his mother, Sylvia.

Roberta mentioned to Carl that divulging Sylvia's address would entail a breach of trust on Roberta's part. However, would he be satisfied with a recent photograph of Sylvia? Reluctantly, he agreed to the compromise. Immediately, Roberta posted a photo of their mother to him. In that photo were Sylvia, her husband, their three daughters, their son, and Roberta. Roberta told Carl that she had taken the photo on Christmas day the previous year.

Carl always looked forward to hearing the news about his biological mother. He also welcomes Roberta's rendition of the family's interactions on her visits to Sylvia's at Christmas, Easter, and Thanksgiving Day each year. Perhaps the cliché that half a loaf of bread is better than no bread at all applies.

Roberta called Sylvia, cautious not to divulge their natural relationship to Sylvia's husband. This compromise worked satisfactorily for some time. However, it is strange how things seem to work themselves out and fall into place with time. Carl hoped that Sylvia's heart would soften and ultimately lead to a mother and son reunion. For a time, all was status quo! But that relationship was about to change.

A year later, Sylvia's husband died from a chronic illness and left his wife to fend for herself. Now, at eighty-nine, Sylvia found it challenging to maintain the vast three-bedroom home they had lived in for the past twenty years. Her inability to drive a vehicle left her at the mercy of others for transportation. A nursing home was not an option unless there was no other alternative.

When Roberta discovered that Sylvia was considering selling her home, she mentioned it to her husband, who suggested they sell their home instead, not Sylvia's. Then Sylvia could live with her biological daughter and remain in the house she loved. Sylvia could have the best of both worlds. She could now be with her daughter and still live in her accustomed manner.

When Roberta proposed the idea to Sylvia, she reluctantly dismissed it as a burden to Roberta. But when Roberta assured Sylvia that it was not an imposition, she accepted the proposal and remained in her home with Roberta and her husband.

One day when Roberta was away buying groceries, Carl called. Sylvia answered the phone, and Carl asked to speak to Roberta. Sylvia mentioned that Roberta was unavailable but would tell her who called.

He said, "Tell Roberta her brother, Carl, called."

Sylvia knew immediately of Carl's relationship with Roberta, and for a moment, there was dead silence. Sylvia had just talked with her son, whom she gave up for adoption sixty years earlier. A mixture of loss, guilt and resolution began to invade her emotions simultaneously.

Without further hesitation, she said, "Carl, Roberta mentioned your name to me when the adoption agency contacted her some time ago. I am Sylvia, your birth mother, with whom you tried communicating some time ago. But Roberta already explained the circumstances to you for my obscurity. With the passing of my husband, the situation has changed. Would you please come to the city at your convenience for a reunion? I live with Roberta and her husband, who take excellent care of me in my declining years."

Carl was stunned to hear such pleasant and assuring words coming from his mother, whom she had refused to acknowledge in the past. But he trusted her sincerity and promised to meet her after he spoke with Roberta.

When Roberta arrived, Sylvia relayed the message about Carl's call. She reiterated the conversation she had with

Carl and the offer of a reunion shortly. Roberta and her husband were elated to know that this family would finally come together amicably. It had been said that to leave home forcefully can be hell, but to return is like heaven.

The Wild Red Mustang

Most of us use the word "trauma" in everyday language to mean a highly stressful event. The media has shown us what happens to soldiers on active duty in combat roles. Extreme stress may cause them to fall into a state of depression. Those who suffer from post-traumatic stress disorder have difficulty coping in life. Some have even committed suicide. However, it is an individual's personal experience that determines whether an event is traumatic. Although Becky was not on active military combat duty, the ordeal she went through was frightening.

Becky, a young, attractive graduate student, concentrated more on her academic studies and less time on socializing. Occasionally, she would go out on a date but did not have a steady boyfriend. With little effort, Becky completed two degrees, a Bachelor of Science and a Bachelor of Education. She reasoned that science was the way of life and the technology of tomorrow. These qualifications helped her to launch a career in pedagogy. She would achieve her main objective in life through science, with vim, vigour and vitality, and a strong ambition to change the world. It did not supersede nor obliterate her religious beliefs but merely served as its utility.

As an added incentive for her academic achievement, her father searched for a graduation gift. At a car dealership, he came across a bright shiny red, used Ford Mustang that Becky would love. The salesman at the car lot spoke highly of this models' popularity.

"This car," he indicated, "comes with an interesting history. The Mustang became part of a woman's divorce settlement after her husband's indiscretion with another woman. He hooked up with a younger woman at work who believed him to be single. His estranged wife mumbled something to the salesman about how he loved the car more than he loved her. To forget about the entire incident, she sold the vehicle to a dealership and moved out of the city, fearing reprisals after the divorce."

The salesman's pitch enticed Becky's father to buy the Mustang.

Becky fell in love with the car the moment she laid eyes on it. She favoured the clean, white leather seats, the stick shift automatic transmission, and the convertible top. Becky took it for a spin to get the feel of the car. As she drove down the streets of the city, the vehicle turned many heads. Young men envied her acquisition, hoping to own a muscle car like it one day.

One bright, warm June morning, Becky felt a nagging urge to test out her pony on the highway. She was curious to see how that Mustang would perform on the open road. So, Becky embarked on a short road trip to Winnipeg. The drive took three and a half hours from her home. She intended to make the return trip in one day. Early that day, she checked her gas gauge and noticed the needle was sitting on FULL. All the horses under the car's hood stood ready to jump into action as she turned the key in the ignition. The motor purred softly like a kitten as she drove out of her garage to the big city. Her Mustang whistled along, silent and smooth into the ceaseless hum of traffic.

Winnipeg is known as the "cultural cradle of Canada," despite its tough-guy image. The city lies in the geographic centre of Canada and North America. The metropolis has bragging rights for having more sunny days than any other Canadian city. Hence the term, "Sunny Manitoba" aptly applies.

As the Mustang sped along the highway, it performed superbly, well beyond all of Becky's expectations. Stable and steady on the road, the ride was fantastic! The sensation was exhilarating as she floated across the prairie as though on a cloud, leaving everyone behind to eat her dust. She bonded with this Mustang, and she made a vow to never part with it.

In her meditation, the time flew by quickly. Before she realized it, the city of Winnipeg came into view. As she cruised down Portage Avenue, she saw Polo Park Shopping Centre.

This mall had a substantial variety of shops serving every individual's needs. Most importantly, it had many ladies' clothing stores catering to women from every walk of life at an affordable price.

At the traffic lights, she signalled and proceeded to the mall. Becky searched for the most suitable parking space nearby. She also searched for vacant spots a comfortable distance from other cars. Proper distancing would ensure no careless driver would accidentally ding her car while opening their door. Even when adequate space is available, it does not resolve the problem with certainty. Fortunately, she found several accessible places to park.

When Becky successfully parked the car and locked it, she proceeded to the mall. Looking back, she noticed a copper-tone Ford Escape slipping into the vacant parking space next to her Mustang, much to her displeasure.

Somewhat disappointed in seeing a car parking next to hers, she continued her mission to the mall.

Entering the building, she looked around for bargains. *I cannot be too extravagant with my purchases until I am offered a teaching position with the school board,* she reasoned.

Becky now focused her attention on finding retail clothing stores with sales to supplant her meagre wardrobe befitting a professional. Several trips around the mall resulted in the purchase of several necessary items. Tired and hungry from all the walking, a light late-afternoon lunch at one of the mall's restaurants soon lifted her spirits.

After lunch, Becky fished the car keys from her purse and returned to her car. To her surprise, the Ford Escape had remained there all this time with the occupant gone. She did not realize the owner of the vehicle also exited the mall simultaneously. Having checked for any dents or markings on her car and finding none, she mellowed and drove out of the parking lot.

While cruising west down Portage Avenue, she checked the rearview mirror before changing lanes. That is when she noticed the same copper-tone Escape following behind. Thinking nothing of the coincidence, she proceeded out of the city on her way home.

Nearing the outskirts of the city, she was puzzled to see the exact vehicle still following her. *Perhaps it will turn off onto the bypass at the exit ramp,* she thought. Continuing west, the Ford suddenly disappeared. She breathed a sigh of relief, relaxed, and calmly settled in for the trip home.

Outside the city limits, the copper-toned Escape again appeared in the mirror. The vehicle accelerated and soon passed her as she accelerated to attain the legal highway cruising speed. The man behind the wheel waved as he passed and motioned for her to stop. She ignored the stranger's request and maintained her cruising speed. Suddenly, the stranger slowed down in front of her. She slipped into the passing lane and wondered if this was a game about to turn into something sinister. However, she kept pushing on.

Two kilometres west of the city, the young man increased his speed, passed her, returned to the driving lane, and decelerated. There was a purposeful, stalking intent in his actions. Despite this aggravation, Becky maintained her self-control, displaying a composed way of handling herself.

The passing and slowing down scenario continued until Becky approached a town twenty minutes east of her home. Stopping at a service station, she called the police and explained her dilemma. According to the law on stalking, the victim must demonstrate that the threat is enough to induce real fear. Since Becky didn't appear to fear the man, the constable advised her to proceed homeward. If the man followed her, he instructed her to report the matter to the city police upon arrival. She was hoping the current stop and the phone call would cause the man to abandon his pursuit. With her stress level now rising after the call, she reluctantly resumed her drive. Back on the highway, the stranger made a U-turn and burned some rubber on the pavement as he spun his tires and kept following her.

Arriving at her hometown, she drove directly to the local police station. Their instructions were to continue driving home. An unmarked police car would follow at a comfortable distance behind, keeping surveillance on her drive home. When she left the police station, the stalker's car was nowhere in sight. With an enormous sigh of relief, her stress level subsided. The constable in the unmarked police car returned to the station, believing the entire problem had ended.

Becky arrived at the apartment she had recently rented, left her car in the parking lot, locked the door, and went to the complex. The entrance door to the foyer always remained open to the public. The main exit from the lobby to the apartment complex locked automatically behind her after she entered.

She took the elevator to her apartment on the second floor, unlocked the door, and went inside. She tried to forget about the incident. After supper, she spent some time on the computer and then went on the treadmill to work out some of the frustrations she had experienced that day. Becky tried desperately to keep the whole episode at a safe distance to put it out of her mind swiftly, but a creeping uneasiness remained in the pit of her stomach.

Then the intercom buzzer announced a visitor at the main door. It startled her, and she hesitated for a moment, uncertain if she should respond. For anyone wanting to visit an occupant in the apartment, it was necessary to contact them by pressing the right room button on an intercom pad in the lobby. When the visitors identified themselves, the occupant would release the lock to let them inside the building.

When Becky finally responded, an unfamiliar male voice asked her if she owned the red Mustang. Since the man did not identify himself, she surmised the stalker had returned. Becky gave him an ultimatum in a teasing tone. If he told her the make of his car, she would answer his question about the red Mustang. When the man told her about his Ford Escape, she quickly called the police and told them about the stalker. No one on duty knew of the previous issue and brushed it off as a hoax. Since Becky did not unlock the door for him, she presumed he had left.

Two minutes later, she heard a gentle knock on her apartment door, and Becky froze. When her composure finally returned, she looked through the peephole in the door and saw Judy, her neighbour, standing there. After Becky let her in, Judy looked shocked to hear about the traumatic experience her neighbour had persevered through that day. Then Judy explained why she knocked on Becky's door. She wanted to know if Becky was selling her beautiful car.

Judy mentioned an encounter her husband had with a man in the parking lot earlier that evening. A young man driving a copper Ford Escape parked in a vacant spot by the complex, and when he spotted her husband, he wanted to know who owned the red Mustang.

"My husband gave him your name. That is how he located your apartment and contacted you on the intercom."

When Judy left, Becky felt rattled, knowing the man now knew her name and where she lived. It would not take long before he got her phone number, and then the calls would come flooding in, filling her answering machine with weird messages. A week later, the man called. He told her how impressed he was seeing someone her age driving such a beautiful car. He suggested going for a ride with her in the Mustang with the top down. The stranger painted a rosy picture of just them two enjoying the beautiful sunny weather together. Becky would allow no one to drive her car and told him to stop harassing her, or she would call the police.

The result of her scorn soon filled the answering machine with messages of jealousy and anger at first, which later turned to spite. She changed her number several times, but he found it each time. She called the police several times, all to no avail. Becky felt murdered in slow motion. The experience was horrifying, and she must do something soon, or she'd lose her mind.

Later that week, the janitor came to Becky and asked her if she knew someone named John Doe. He mentioned being a close friend who just returned from a business trip and lost his passkey. He told Becky that after she left to visit her parents for the weekend, this man offered him two hundred dollars for the key to her apartment. The janitor said he would require permission from the occupant to release a key. The man grew angry and squealed his tires as he left, almost hitting another vehicle on the way out.

Becky told the janitor about the stalking incident and thanked him for not releasing the key. After the janitor left, she feared that the stalker would go to any length to get closer to her.

Then, just as suddenly as the whole ordeal began, it abruptly stopped. There were no more phone calls, nor any disturbing messages on the answering machine. Becky thought the man was devising some complex evil scheme to harass her. But, after the last police call about the key incident, there was silence until that evening.

The reporter on the local news that evening reported a tragic automobile accident on the highway. A copper-tone Ford Escape SUV collided with a semi at an intersection. Half of the SUV ended up under the trailer of the semi. The sole occupant of the vehicle died instantly. Now Becky knew why the harassment had stopped.

Stalking is a rare phenomenon and not taken seriously. However, psychologists say that people who are being stalked repeatedly feel they have little control and experience longer-lasting distress. It could be anxiety and depression or more immediate panic and insomnia.

Fortunately, this disturbing incident had a minor effect on her psychic and did not impair Becky's ability to cope. However, this terrifying time is still locked deep inside. Whenever the mind flashes back to the events of that grim day, she shudders when recalling the frightening occurrence and how it affected her emotionally. Eventually, she sold the Mustang, despite the fact that she had vowed to keep it and never sell it.

She explained her reason for selling it by saying, "Out of sight, out of mind!"

A Celiac's Burden

Good food, wine, and a candlelight atmosphere symbolize a divine respite. Dining together for two hours offers ample time to enjoy the food and engage in meaningful conversation with your companion. Today, eateries offer fast-food services to those that have no time to sit down and eat. These people in our society's fast lane have often utilized these services but at a heavy price. Obesity and eating disorders have negatively affected their lives. Digestive problems have become a common complaint at medical clinics these days.

Several years into their marriage, Colin's wife, Joan, experienced frequent stomach aches and indigestion problems. This sudden onset of discomfort caused Colin to wonder if he precipitated her condition or whether food caused her gastric disorder. To dispel that uneasy feeling that somehow he had caused her sickness, Colin observed the frequency of her distress before discomfort set in. He noticed the symptoms occurred after eating a sandwich, pasta, or indulging in a toasted cinnamon bun smothered with butter. It was cold relief to discover the food she ate caused her digestive problem and not their marriage! But Joan always dealt with pain on her own by chewing several antacid tablets. After several minutes, the pain would slowly subside. This treatment continued for several years.

However, when the couple moved to another city, her illness became more severe. Finally, Joan sought medical assistance to correct the problem.

At her next medical appointment, she mentioned the ailment to her practitioner. With just one look at Joan's pallid face, the doctor suspected her anemic condition stemmed from a lack of iron in her system. He explained that an allergic reaction to gluten would cause an iron deficiency. The culprits are the proteins we find in wheat and related grains, including barley, rye, and their species and hybrids. Gluten retains viscoelastic properties necessary in baking bread.

The doctor presumed that the element causing Joan all that pain was the gluten in the foods she ate. After undergoing several laboratory tests to confirm his suspicions, the physician recommended that Joan avoid any foods containing wheat, barley, or rye. He asserted these grains had gluten and were the cause of her pain. People with celiac disease suffer from a severe allergic reaction if they consume any gluten. The intestines prevent the body from absorbing nutrients, minerals, and fat-soluble vitamins A, D, E, and K.

When Joan returned home from her medical appointment, she quickly purged every glutenous food from her pantry. All the enjoyable foods containing gluten also disappeared from Colin's menu. Pasta, pizza, perogies, bread, and pastry—all the good stuff got the heave-ho to never, never land! However, this annoyance was only the tip of the iceberg. Soon, other problems reared their ugly heads, especially when travelling.

Some months following the diagnosis, dining out became a concern as they travelled to other towns and cities on appointments or vacations. The couple discovered that many restaurant servers had no training in serving customers with this allergy. Joan found it disturbing to see how little the servers in dining places knew about gluten and its sources. Often, when asked if a particular food was gluten-free, some drew a blank look and were unresponsive. When questioned about specific entrees on the menu, the reply was, "It should be gluten-free," even though their knowledge of it was limited or even nonexistent.

When ordering a main course at an upscale restaurant one day, the server assured Joan that the prime rib was gluten-free. Confidence in the waitress' words of assurance, she placed her order. When the plate came to the table, she confidently ate.

Suddenly, the server rushed back to the table and advised her to stop eating the roast beef immediately because the au jus dipping sauce contained gluten. Unfortunately, she had ingested some of it, and the unpleasantness of excruciating pain and discomfort would follow. The waitress explained the reason for the error as a miscommunication between the chef and the server.

Returning home, she sat curled up in a comfortable chair, waiting for the pain to subside. While suffering patiently with the discomfort, her mind flashed back to her teen years when food allergies were rare and difficult to diagnose. In researching this topic, she discovered that modern wheat differs significantly from what it was thousands of years ago. It differs even from what it was in the twentieth century. Due to crossbreeding over many years, modern wheat's composition went through a transformation. Today, it is about two feet tall with large seeds, whereas before, it was much taller. Gluten's structure in modern wheat changed somewhat. Modern wheat also contains higher levels of the starch Amylopectin A. Some research suggests that wheat's alteration has something to do with gluten sensitivity.

Further study revealed that in the early nineteenth century, an era fondly called the "good old days," travel took a lot of time from one place to another. When pioneers travelled away from home, a ring of garlic sausage and a loaf of bread sufficed for a quick fix when hunger struck. However, with the invention of powerful automobiles, travel became more prevalent. Dining out in eateries and restaurants became popular as society became more affluent. With a rise in the standard of living came an increase in allergies. Researchers estimate that 1 in 133 Americans have celiac disease or about 1 percent of the population. No one had heard of this condition then.

As doctors diagnose more patients with this illness, servers and chefs must learn of this allergy. It should be mandatory for all food handlers to undergo a training program that educates restaurant personnel. The training is necessary for the entire restaurant staff. They must understand the severity of all food allergies and the precautions to be taken. Sometimes, this is sorely lacking.

For example, a humiliating incident occurred recently while on their travels to a nearby city. Colin and Joan ventured into a restaurant for lunch that day. As they waited in the foyer for the hostess to escort them to a table, Joan asked her if they had anything on the menu that was gluten-free.

Much to their embarrassment, she replied, "We serve nothing here that is free."

When they finally overcame the embarrassment, Colin assured the hostess that they were not looking for a free meal. He explained that Joan was allergic to gluten and wondered if they served any meals without gluten in them. Suddenly, the server felt the same awkwardness the couple had experienced, but for a different reason. Today, some diners have renamed the term "gluten-free" foods to "gluten-aware" to avoid such embarrassing situations.

On another occasion, a meat handler at a grocery store displayed his lack of knowledge about this allergy. It was midsummer, and the barbeque season was at its peak. Colin and Joan were about to purchase hamburger patties at a local grocery store. From Joan's experience, hamburger patties were prepared with breadcrumbs as a binder to hold the meat together. Some use no binder, just pure beef. Others use rolled oats to accommodate celiac sufferers. When purchasing hamburger patties without the breadcrumb binder, ingesting the meat produced no discomfort. Informing the butcher about her gluten allergy, she asked him to direct her to the patties that would be safe.

Much to her surprise, he explained, "If cattle are grain-fed with wheat, barley, or rye, the gluten is absorbed into the meat and is therefore not gluten-free. Only meat from grass-fed animals can be safely ingested by celiac suffers."

They thought this was ludicrous! On several occasions, they had purchased steaks or roasts of grain-fed cattle with no gastric discomfort. Colin struggled with the temptation to inquire if the milk and eggs also contained gluten but resisted. In frustration, Joan emptied her shopping cart of all the food products she gathered, crossed the street to another grocery store and purchased the same products. This grocer was more knowledgeable of his produce and the ingredients they contained.

The couple learned of this fallacy of gluten absorption in meat before this incident.

A registered dietitian and gluten-free expert, Tricia Thompson, MSRD, explained that "Grain-fed beef is fine. Before protein is absorbed, it's broken down into single amino acids or very short peptide fragments, thereby no longer gluten."

It was a fact the butcher did not know!

For those with celiac disease, restaurant dining is challenging. Purchasing food at the grocery store requires much patience and constant checking of ingredients on labels. Therefore, it always was, and still is, an ordeal whenever ordering a meal at a restaurant or buying products at a grocery store.

In restaurants, Colin always cringes when the server approaches and asks for their order. Often, the menu contains no palatable gluten-free choices. In anticipation of this, Joan must "pre-eat" before dining out, so her hunger is under control, and avoid the temptation to make unsafe menu choices. Then, there is always a risk of cross-contamination in restaurant kitchens, even though it is labelled safe.

When Joan unintentionally ingests foods with gluten, a feeling of uneasiness spiced with irritation develops within her. For Joan, it is an evening of grey unrest as the pain and discomfort settle in. Lying in bed in a fetal position wrapped in a blanket, she remains there for several hours until the problem runs its course. Such are the concerns that await a celiac if they neglect taking precautions to avoid the excruciating pain.

In later years, more gluten-free items were available for purchase at grocery stores and bakeries. A special section had a gluten-free label drawing the customer's attention to the product. But, adding insult to injury, the price doubled in comparison to the regular item.

However, on the positive side, removing bread, cupcakes, and pasta from your diet may help you lose weight, even though it is not directly attributed to gluten.

All Bad Things Come in Threes

It is common knowledge that the universe operates on the laws of nature. These laws apply to everyone, and breaking them can be disastrous. Dan and Susan lived through some unfortunate occurrences in the early part of their adult lives, and the memory of this time will remain with them for many years to come.

Dan and Susan attended the same elementary school since the first grade. Their parents lived at opposite ends of the same school district in a small city. Most children at that age form gendered cliques. Boys hang around with boys and girls with girls, but these dynamics change in high school. Boys suddenly notice girls and vice versa. When Dan started Grade 10, he would surreptitiously glance over at Susan while she was busy concentrating on her assignment. Once Dan overcame his shyness, he boldly struck up a conversation with Susan. Eventually, he asked her on a date. She accepted. They dated throughout the remainder of their school years. After receiving their high school diplomas, both spent most of their free time together.

With little money available for college, both sought employment in the city. Susan obtained a serving position at a local eatery, while Dan became a stock boy in a grocery store. Within six months of training, the manager elevated Dan to a produce manager. The work was fulfilling and enjoyable, making him proud of his accomplishment. He, being a thrifty young man, had saved much of his earnings for a particular reason.

Then one day, on bended knee, Dan asked Susan to marry him. Following her acceptance, wedding plans went into motion. When Dan's friends heard of the impending marriage, they agreed to throw him a huge stag party with all the trimmings.

After some discussion amongst Dan's friends, they considered reserving a nightclub for the occasion. It would be the perfect venue for a bachelor party. The dedicated, experienced chefs and the front of house staff would ensure an enjoyable bash.

Several manly functions flashed through their minds before the celebration. One friend suggested an exciting activity, waging an epic archery tag battle for physical fun before the wedding.

The second option involved playing an escape room game. What an excellent way, they thought, to introduce a groom to the confines of marriage with an escape room? This game would be a perfect option for the husband-to-be as an exciting mental workout before the wedding's exhausting emotional workout.

A third option they considered was attempting some potentially death-defying feats while drinking lots of beer. It would test the groom's limits differently with outdoor activities like whitewater rafting, skydiving, hang-gliding or bungee jumping. When the jam-packed day ended, they could share embarrassing stories about the groom's high school adventures.

Since the lack of proper planning can cause a miserable bachelor party experience, they chose the third option and went whitewater rafting. The venue would end at the bistro with food and sharing stories. For the finale, a bikini-clad girl would entertain them with a dance.

The restaurant hired a young attractive college girl in her early twenties, with lips that drooped sensuously at each corner and delicate, silky eyebrows that rose a trifle. She was in her second year at university and required additional money for sundry expenses. Student loans took care of tuition fees and accommodations for the year, but not the incidentals. It was necessary to obtain temporary employment to supplement her income. Waiting on tables was not her forte, an endeavour most students favoured. She preferred something less taxing but more lucrative in the entertainment field.

Early in her teens, Amy had discovered her alluring ways. She was beautiful and gifted with an hourglass figure. This girl possessed attributes that made her a suitable candidate for such an undertaking, not as a bar stripper, but a dancer! She would come on stage for several minutes, do her dance and then depart. It was leisurely work with substantial earnings. Her first assignment was to entertain at Dan's stag party.

By the river, meanwhile, after a few beers, the men were having a hilarious time whitewater rafting until a near-tragedy struck. Shayne, a bachelor party reveller, was shaken when the raft Dan and Shayne were in, along with a river guide, capsized after hitting a boulder. A strong current pinned Shayne under what rafters call an "undercut rock," formed by strong winds consistently smashing water into the riverbed rocks. Thankfully, the capable guide rescued him. Somewhat distraught about the unfortunate incident, he regained his composure and carried on with the party. The others jovially mocked him as they left the area. He took it lightheartedly and shrugged it off.

After the mishap, the group proceeded to the lounge for food and more drinks. Upon Dan's request, only female servers must work at the party. The problem began when one of Dan's friends, Silas, had consumed too much alcohol, putting a damper on their celebration. After serving him another drink, the server turned her back to leave. Silas quickly and involuntarily purged much of what he consumed onto her bare back. The gushing liquid startled the server, causing her to let out a loud, ear-piercing shriek.

The waitress lost her balance and sent her tray with empty glasses flying across the room toward Dan. The groom was consoling Shayne after his rafting scare and was unaware of the empty glasses hurling toward him. One of the glasses caught Dan in the eye, leaving him with a red mark that later turned into a black eye. Meanwhile, the server regained her composure and rushed to the bathroom to clean up. After that incident, she reconsidered her employment choices.

The party continued into the night, drinking beer, and telling stories. The men were in a cheerful mood from alcohol consumption. Then the entertainment coordinator of the restaurant introduced the dancer. The stage lights came on, and suddenly everyone diverted their eyes to the enormous cake.

A tap on the stage floor, pre-arranged by the organizer, signalled the girl's cue to jump out of the cake and surprise everyone. Tap. Tap. Tap. Nothing happened! He tapped once more, but still no response. The men showed concern when the dancer failed to pop out through the top layer of the cake.

"Perhaps she's not there," they wondered.

The banquet organizer assured them that a girl inside was waiting for the signal to pop out.

The signal was repeated a little harder this time, with a similar response. Finally, the man cut open the cake to find Amy still inside. What a horrible surprise they got when they saw the young dancer unresponsive. Amy was rushed to the hospital and eventually recovered. The college student had taken a pill laced with fentanyl. The stag party took on a sombre note following the discovery of the young girl's unfortunate outcome. Although Dan and his friends were disappointed with the stag's entertainment portion, they were genuinely remorseful for the near-tragic outcome of the event.

The following day, after an evening of excessive drinking, some of Dan's friends were hungover. Most were tired, thirsty, nauseous, and enduring headaches, muscle aches, and a black eye. Dan, however, who was not a drinker, remained sober throughout the party. That day, the couple had an appointment with the caterers, and Dan did not want to find himself inside the four walls of a hospital ward.

After making all the arrangements for the wedding, the most important day of their lives finally arrived. All their relatives gathered for the ceremony. Before the Justice of the Peace, the couple exchanged their vows and were united in marriage. The three unfortunate events that happened before their union vanished from their memory. They were beginning a new chapter in their lives. Their married life started with the romantic custom of the groom carrying his bride over the threshold into their new home. The following day, they packed some of their belongings and set out on their honeymoon.

During their courtship, Susan met Dan's mother and father twice and only for a short time. When his parents discovered a Justice of the Peace wedding, it greatly upset his mother. Despite their disappointment, the groom's mother and father offered to pay for a fancy honeymoon to Niagara Falls, Ontario to compensate for their lack of involvement. This generous offer elated Susan, for they had little money for such an elegant retreat.

The couple arrived at the hotel and proceeded to their room. That evening, they went out to an upscale restaurant nearby for supper. The host escorted them to a cozy table for two. While they were enjoying their meal, another couple arrived and were seated some distance from them. On closer observation, Susan felt as though she knew them. Suddenly a light came on, and she realized it was her in-laws.

The groom's parents had treated themselves to a holiday and stayed in the same hotel, just one door down. Worst of all, the groom's mother and father got into a heated argument, and she didn't feel like going back to their room. Instead, she wanted to spend the night in her son and new daughter-in-law's room.

When Dan asked his mother to leave, she became belligerent and replied, "How could you do this to your mother! I paid for this room. It's only for tonight." She added, "If you don't let me stay, you can both get out!"

The couple couldn't afford to honeymoon anywhere else, so the groom felt compelled to let her stay.

Several weeks later, another misfortune befell them. Dan's Uncle Bill was out in the garden one morning. Early mornings were an excellent time to work before the morning sun became too hot for the tedious task of weeding. He was busy at work, making remarkable progress ridding his garden of noxious weeds. After toiling for an hour, he stopped to look at the progress he was making. At that moment, he felt an unusual pain in his chest. Perhaps it was a touch of indigestion, he thought! However, the problem continued and became more intense. He called out to his wife, Mabel, and indicated that he was having difficulty breathing. She immediately sensed a medical emergency and dialled 911 for the ambulance.

In a few minutes, the ambulance arrived and checked Bill over. They gave him an injection and placed him on a respirator. He was strapped down to the stretcher and wheeled out of the house to the waiting ambulance.

The driveway to the house was on a slight incline. Since the patient was highly agitated, the physician on duty assisted the paramedics via a two-way radio. With their attention averted, the gurney rolled away. Suddenly, a loud crash pierced the air from the street below, which startled the attendants. The oncoming car collided with the free-wheeling stretcher and flipped it on its side, patient and all. The cot finally came to rest fifty feet from the driveway. The paramedics raced down the incline, quickly retrieved the stretcher, and rushed the patient to the hospital. Bill had suffered internal injuries, and after a lengthy stay in the hospital, was released. Dan and Susan were thankful for his recovery, for Dan was fond of his Uncle Bill.

To complete the second trio of unfortunate happenings, this time, Susan's brother was involved. Tony was a sales representative for an animal feed company. His occupation as a travelling salesman kept him away from home for several days a week. On this day, Tony travelled on a major highway between two small cities for about twenty-three kilometres. A short distance from his destination, his cell phone buzzed in his pocket. When he retrieved the phone, he noticed a text message from his wife, Bianca. Being a curious sort and desperate to know what she had written, he opened her text message. With one eye on the road and the other on the cell phone, he read her message. The information must have been alarming, for suddenly, both eyes shifted from the highway and became glued to the phone.

He was travelling at a legal speed, following several cars. Oblivious to Tony, they were approaching the junction of a side road. When the vehicle ahead was approximately twenty yards away from the intersection, the driver slowed down to execute a right turn. However, with both eyes focused on the cellphone, Tony was unaware that the car in front had its proper signal flashing and reducing its speed. All at once, there was an earth-shattering crash of steel on steel. Tony had rear-ended the car in front of him and sent it careening into the ditch. The ambulance arrived and took both drivers to the hospital for a thorough examination. Fortunately, both drivers sustained no significant injuries. Tony, however, received a citation for careless driving.

Dan and Susan's memory of these unfortunate events, three before and three at the onset of their married life, was a dim reminder that tragedy could strike without warning. Death and injuries have no respect for time, place, or person.

Young adults are always ready to take risks for fun. Sometimes, however, such attempts create a disaster for others. Barring any fatalities, we eventually reach a stage where we can look back and see all the foolish things we did and wish that somehow, we had known then what we know now. Our life would be so much better had we just learned those lessons earlier and prevented all that grief! For those whose errors resulted in their demise, the warning will always be there as a valuable lesson for others.

Heroes and Villains in a Crisis

When the Coronavirus pandemic hit Canada in March of 2020, life gradually slowed down to a crawl. That is the way it always is when a crisis arises. Everything is put on hold until the affected people resolve the problem and life returns to normal. When he discovered how this crisis originated and the turmoil it created, it made Homer angry. He was grateful and pleased with his recent promotion to an administrative position but suspected this pandemic was about to put a damper on his career.

Within three weeks of the virus' arrival in the country, it created a domino effect, and infections were running rampant. Consequently, Homer and his wife, Daisy, became unemployed. The severity of this disease gave them cause to worry. In this family, there were two adults and two children to feed and clothe. Mortgage payments would keep coming each month despite their loss of income. As some scientists predicted, he wondered how they would survive if this pandemic lasted for six months. He prayed someone would soon discover a vaccine or an effective antiviral treatment to halt Coronavirus from spreading. It was a waiting game.

Since the onset, the media was providing daily coverage of the virus. Homer discovered that this deadly virus had originated in Wuhan, China, in late December 2019. He was unfamiliar with that name until the media brought it into the spotlight, and the Coronavirus made headlines worldwide.

Scientists believed that bat meat sold at wild animal markets in that city had sparked this virus' outbreak. Others suspected that scientists had developed this deadly strain in a laboratory but not for biological warfare. However, scientists named it Covid-19 to indicate its appearance in 2019. At the outset, had the infected people remained isolated, the virus would not have affected the global community. The respiratory droplets of an infected person spread rapidly when they coughed, sneezed, or talked near someone. Understandably, Homer was not a happy man!

Homer recalled that in previous years, similar viruses surfaced. There was SARS, the Swine Flu and H1N1, to name a few. They were also a severe health risk to the public but not considered as lethal as the current one. He knew that other viruses would continue to pop up regularly until they discovered the root of the problem. He felt there was no alternative but to deal with this crisis by going with the flow until then.

Meanwhile, pertinent information was necessary to avoid becoming its victim. Promptly, the federal government stepped in with some directives. Since this disease was so new to them, many directions arose on the basis of trial and error.

Politicians and doctors urged the public to maintain social distancing of at least two metres or six feet to prevent contracting this disease. Later, the distance was increased to four metres or twelve feet by some doctors. The chief public health officer prescribed wearing masks in public gatherings, hand washing, regularly sanitizing hands, and avoiding touching the face.

After presenting these restrictions to the public, businesses shut down, and unemployment statistics rose to acute heights. When businesses closed, the stock markets dipped to critically low levels. This reaction resulted in layoffs and quarantines. It became a challenge to combat the virus with a faltering economy. On a positive note, life slowed down to a level where people could stop and smell the roses. However, not everyone was happy with solitude for extended periods.

Homer, too, was getting listless and bored from being cooped up at home for more than a week. The family was running short of groceries, so Homer drove to the local grocery store to replenish them. Turning into the store parking lot, he wondered why so many cars were there, considering the provincial government had restricted large gatherings. As he approached the store's entrance, he noticed a lineup of people standing two metres apart, queued up outside waiting to enter. A maximum of fifty people were allowed in one location simultaneously. As one shopper completed the purchase and left by another door, the greeter ushered in the next patron.

Homer waited in line for what seemed like an hour before being allowed to enter. He was glad the establishment was following the safety rules to protect their customers. So, he grabbed a cart in the foyer, sanitized the handle with the provided wipes, and entered the store. At the entrance and strategically placed throughout the store, were arrows marking the direction customers must follow to maintain their social distancing. Some customers did not follow the flow and were passing each other in the narrow aisles. Despite all the rules provided for the customers' safety, they were useless if patrons neglected to follow them.

Therefore, the government went into a persuasive mode, pointing out that we're all in this together. Still, this fell on deaf ears. Not everyone was accepting it. The federal government then invoked the Quarantine Act with the threat of fines and jail time for those who disobey orders to isolate following travel from outside the country. Imposing penalties became a deterrent for those who did not maintain social distancing. It was difficult for Homer to understand why people would ignore these rules and needlessly risk their lives and the lives of others. Someone once said, "You can't fix stupid!" But not everyone falls into this category.

In difficult times, many people struggle to stay alive. Hailed as heroes were those unaffected people who chose to help others to the best of their abilities. But then others showed their true colours. We encounter both heroes and villains in practically every walk of life. During this pandemic, it was no different. An example of heartlessness came from the hotel owner of Britannia Hotels, headquartered in Hale, Manchester. Britannia Hotels had fired all their employees and targeted those with accommodation included with their job. It left them homeless. But there was more!

The government's call for school closures and social support services affected many people working with abused children. The closures placed children at high risk. Many parents and childcare workers said kids were agitated by these changes. Agencies that serve abused children were expecting an increase in abuse cases. This lack of concern for others also affected the police service.

A devastating blow was felt by the citizens of Nova Scotia when Gabriel Wortman went on a gun rampage across the northern part of that province, killing twenty-two citizens of several rural communities. On Saturday, April 18, and Sunday morning, he became notorious for the deadliest killing spree in modern Canadian history. All this was happening while Covid-19 was still running rampant.

Some politicians were no different when pushing their agenda into the mix. Alberta graciously offered to donate up to 761 ventilators from their surplus to other provinces that needed them. However, the premier's offer became tainted with a quid pro quo favour. In addressing the press, the premier said, "We are all in this together, and the same should apply to the energy sector." He was referring to the stalled pipeline.

Deserting the needy had crushed Homer's faith in humanity when he heard about some nurses abandoning several nursing homes and leaving seniors helpless and unattended for several days. When authorities arrived two days later, following complaints that some seniors had died, others were malnourished, and some were lying in urine and feces in their beds, an investigation ensued to determine who was to blame for this atrocity. The staff's criticism focused on a lack of personal protective equipment necessary to work safely in the establishment, so they left.

Also topping Homer's villain list were the individuals who had bought up all the hand sanitizers they could find and tried reselling them on eBay at a profit of one thousand percent. And then there were the hoarders who emptied store shelves of toilet paper, leaving the rest of the community searching for other alternatives.

Despite all these negative actions, what inspired Homer were stories of people's sacrifices to help those in need. Many Good Samaritans displayed care and concern for others, helping ease their distress and fears under challenging times. These were the first responders, the cashiers at grocery stores and pharmacies, the men and women who deliver groceries to the elderly and physically challenged. There was holiness in their work.

Likewise, there was something sacred in the work of doctors, nurses, technicians, and hospital staff when they put their well-being and families at risk. They were the true heroes in Homer's mind. Unfortunately, several doctors and nurses contracted the virus while on duty and succumbed to their illness. Due to the public's negligence in following safety rules, emergency wards become flooded with patients. This influx of patients created a shortage of personal protective equipment and placed the caregiver's life in jeopardy. The lack of concern for others was demoralizing, but as examples of self-sacrifice emerged, it restored Homer's faith in humanity. He hoped those who died by giving their lives for others would inspire everyone to emulate them and serve as an example of profound charity.

An Italian Catholic priest from Lovere displayed an act of true heroism. Father Giuseppe Berardelli, seventy-two, had contracted the Coronavirus while it spread rampantly in Italy in March of 2020. So, Father Giuseppe's parishioners bought him a respirator, but he refused the lifesaving gift and requested it go to a younger patient, whom he did not know. Father Giuseppe died at the hospital in Lovere, where he was undergoing treatment. He sacrificed himself for another.

A glimmer of hope came to Homer when he heard that the federal government would help businesses keep and return workers to their payroll. The prime minister proposed the new Emergency Wage Subsidy, which would provide a 75 percent wage subsidy to eligible employers for up to twelve weeks, retroactive to March 15, 2020. This wage subsidy would discourage further job losses by encouraging employers to rehire workers who were laid off because of Covid-19. It would help Canadian companies and other employers to resume normal operations more quickly following the crisis. But this came with the understanding that employers use the subsidy to support their employees' health and well-being.

When Homer learned of this, it was like a lottery win. He and his family were ecstatic. He could resume his administrative position, and his wife could return to her previous place of employment.

While waiting for the money from the subsidies to flow so his wife could return to work, Homer thought of ways he and his family could help those in need. They were fortunate enough to be free of the virus and wanted to support their community in some beneficial way. He took stock of himself to determine what attributes would help the needy in the city.

Homer was an economics professor, recently promoted to dean of the university. His students were in their last year of study before graduation. Since classes were closed indefinitely due to the pandemic, students would not graduate this year. So, he arranged a Zoom conference with the other professors and suggested they agree to teach their classes from home via online video conferencing. Since every student had a computer at home, they could all tune in to the lessons at a designated time. Each professor agreed to try that method, and it worked. Their students could complete all their courses and graduate. Since the economy had floundered during the pandemic, it would need fresh minds and brains to jump-start it again.

Fairytale stories always conclude with happy endings. In them, the good still overpowers the bad, and everyone lives happily ever after. That might sit well with children, but that's not reality! When we observe the grief and loneliness this virus created for seniors dying alone in nursing homes, restricted from having their family present, there is no happy ending. The happy ending comes after people have lived their lives righteously here on earth. Only the resurrection miracle assures them a paradise in heaven.

Haunted House for Rent

In chapter twenty-eight of Adrian P. Cooper's book, *Our Ultimate Reality*, the chapter deals with "The Truth about Ghosts and Haunted Houses." He writes that a "ghost" is a person who died but was strongly attracted to this world and wished to remain here. This attraction motivates the ghost to draw cosmic energy from its surroundings at will. This energy keeps them here in an etheric body rather than transporting them to the astral world. The soul of a deceased person stays in one location, a house, for example, as a "ghost." The place is said to be "haunted" and spooky. Such sites can be frightening to children and those who have never encountered a ghost."

When young adults leave the comfort of their parent's homes, the move can be bittersweet. Leaving the nest brings many new experiences in life, some of which are scary. Such was Stanley's dilemma.

To Stanley, an up-and-coming educator, ghosts were merely imaginary beings created by parents to keep their children under control using the child's fear. Stanley grew up in the latter part of the twentieth century and had no knowledge of the paranormal. That lack of experience would soon become apparent.

Immediately after graduation, Stanley applied for suitable teaching positions advertised in the newspaper. After responding to many advertisements, he attracted an interested school division. The superintendent scheduled a phone interview for Stanley.

The comprehensive interview lasted thirty minutes. Much to Stanley's surprise, he was offered an administrative position in an elementary school. This position amazed him, for he had no experience in administration.

The position would take him to a remote village in the north. The superintendent was cautious in presenting Stanley with some negative factors he would be facing in the community. Not wanting to discourage the applicant from accepting the position but still being truthful, the superintendent informed Stanley that finding suitable accommodations and other amenities in the village would be a challenge but not impossible.

Although there was a shortage of suitable housing in that community, one vacant house was available. However, there was a stigma attached to the empty residence. The locals called it a haunted house. A second but more appealing option was to commute from a town fourteen kilometres away. This location offered a better choice of accommodations but meant costly travel expenses and treacherous road conditions in winter.

A further deterrent was the employee's responsibility to be on duty during inclement weather. If absent on such occasions, a salary deduction would be applied equal to the number of days absent. Mulling over the information and despite several disadvantages to the offer, he accepted the position.

Stan's main concern was the housing availability issue. He wondered if he should drive the fourteen kilometres to work each day or rent the haunted house in the community. The dilemma persuaded him to question his father about haunted houses. He was curious whether ghosts were a figment of someone's imagination or if there was some truth to the existence of paranormal entities. His father offered no concrete evidence on this topic and showed skepticism of any metaphysical existence.

During the summer break, Stan began a thorough library search on haunted houses. Much to his chagrin, he discovered reports of countless ghost stories in Canada alone. For example, at the Banff Springs Hotel, a young bride descended the marble staircase on her wedding day. Beautiful candles highlighted the stairway on this special occasion. As she came down the stairs, the train of her wedding dress accidentally caught fire. The bride panicked and tumbled down the stairs, breaking her neck. To this day, some say a ghost in a wedding dress wanders through the halls of the hotel. When this became known, management blocked the stairs and discontinued other weddings in that area of the hotel.

Another article carried a story from Brandon, Manitoba. When the Art Gallery of Southwestern Manitoba was vacant, the night cleaners would hear footsteps in the building. An eerie feeling, as though someone was watching, was frightening the people away. Stan discovered similar stories with weird feelings that accompanied them.

What Stan needed was objective proof. Hearing and reading differed from experience. The more he thought about it, the more intrigued he became with encountering an apparition. He had visions of accosting a ghost, and it seemed to be generating a strong desire in him to rent the house.

Several days before the school year began, Stan approached Ben, the homeowner, about renting his haunted house. He assured Stan it was vacant and available for lease.

Being curious about its present status, Stan asked why it was unoccupied.

"Well, Stan," Ben said, "several years ago, a young man committed suicide there. Before that tragedy, the man's wife became unhappy with her lot, packed up her belongings and boarded the first bus out of town. The man became so distraught when she left that he took his own life. Ever since that tragic incident, strange unexplainable noises came from within the house at midnight. The locals assume the suicide occurred at approximately that time."

He continued, "One day, an intoxicated man staggered into the house to sober up. I always left the door unlocked. Suddenly, strange sights and eerie noises began attacking him. His legs quickly found enough stability to jet propel him from the house in a hurry. He left there cursing and screaming at the top of his lungs. Later, he claimed elephants and snakes were crawling out of the walls and emitting weird noises."

Stanley knew that anyone who has lived with an alcoholic was aware of a condition called delirium tremens. This condition typically only occurred in people with a high intake of alcohol for more than a month. Physical effects might include seeing or hearing things other people do not. This alcoholic experienced the impact of excessive drinking and not a ghost. Stan assumed this caused the man's reactions.

Ben ended his explanation by saying, "Several neighbours were claiming they caught sight of a ghost parading through the house at midnight, calling for his wife to come back. They alleged the voice was very eerie but audible. I'm telling you this so that you will know what you are leasing."

"Thank you, Ben, for being so honest with me," Stan replied. "However, I am skeptical about the existence of ghosts. Therefore, to prove to myself that this is a myth and a figment of people's imagination, I would like to rent the house."

Stan moved in the next day and hung a crucifix at the entrance. It was the custom at his father's house to have a cross hanging above the entrance door. Filled with great anticipation, he hoped to disprove the stories about apparitions. As evening approached, a feeling of apprehension crept in. He desperately tried to convince himself that if there was such a thing as a manifestation, what harm could a ghost inflict upon a human? It was just an apparition!

The dictionary defines the word "ghost" as the *supposed* spirit of somebody who has died. Stanley reasoned the word "*supposed*" indicated doubt. His search revealed no indication that a ghost had ever harmed any living being. So, what is there to fear but fear itself?

Midnight came and went. Nothing happened! There were no strange sounds, no shadowy forms floating through closed doors. The same scenario played itself out every night without incident.

At the end of the school year, Stan obtained a teaching position closer to home. Several months later, he called Ben to inquire about the house. Ben could not understand why the apparition had abandoned the house during Stan's stay. Ben vowed it was a conundrum. However, since then, he assumed the ghost had returned due to the strange noises emanating from the house every night once again.

As Stan reflected on his experience in that house, he wondered if the apparition's return had something to do with the removal of the blessed crucifix from above the entrance when he moved out. Or perhaps some people have a vivid imagination and are easily overwhelmed by things that frighten them.

Many people fear ghosts simply because they lack enough knowledge about them. Few people understand and know how to protect themselves from them. Although things unknown and mysterious are scary, they still pique one's curiosity, and people formulate their own opinions of ghosts. It provides fodder for writers and playwrights.

To this day, Stanley claims he has never seen a ghost, nor has he ever been to a house where supposedly a spirit was making strange noises, switching lights on and off, or rattling pots and pans. He has, however, been to a musical production called *The Phantom of the Opera*. That is one of his favourite theatre productions and the only phantom he cares to see.

FAITH

Our Guardian Angel

How long have you been waiting for a divine sign in your life? Through baptism, a guardian angel is assigned to all of us to guide and protect us. However, most people are unaware that guardian angels exist until a situation occurs that is life-threatening. In times of danger, our guardian angel is close by, guiding and protecting us from misfortunes as we struggle through life's challenges.

For those who are skeptical, guardian angels are not a figment of one's imagination. The Holy Bible explicitly mentions them. "See, I am sending an angel before you to guard you on the way and bring you to the place I have prepared. Be attentive to him and heed his voice. Do not rebel against him, for he will not forgive your sin. My authority resides in him. If you heed his voice and carry out all I tell you, I will be an enemy to your enemies and a foe to your foes." (Ex 23:20–22)

Jack recalls how often his guardian angel protected him from tragic consequences. The first meaningful encounter with this divine sign was at age fifteen. When Jack graduated from junior high, he applied for summer employment with the local plumbing contractor in the small village where his parents resided.

One day, some community residents went to the municipal office to complain about their local water supply. The pump would only supply enough water to anyone strong enough to manipulate the pump's handle and only if it worked correctly. But the pump malfunctioned and left them without drinking water. Despite all their efforts, not a drop of water rose from the well. The following day, plumbers arrived at the community well to repair the hand pump's malfunctioning apparatus. Upon their arrival, the men noticed that a small shed housed this pump.

After a brief inspection, they determined that the problem was at the bottom of the pipe, deep inside the well. To access that part of the unit would require lifting both pump and pipes upward simultaneously and projecting it through a small opening in the roof. Jack climbed on top of the building by a side ladder. Once there, he needed to guide the unit through a small gap by keeping the pump-head perpendicular to the roof. This method would prevent damage to the building's roof when he lowered it back into the building.

Inside the shed, the contractor was slowly lifting the pump out of the well. As it inched its way out, Jack carefully guided and steadied it along its route. When the ascent stopped, the contractor inspected the pipe, looking for the problem. As he was checking, suddenly and unexpectedly, the unit slipped out of the contractor's hands and came crashing down. The protruding spout of the pump snagged part of the ceiling on its way down and shattered it. Luckily, the spout pointed away from Jack, or it would have come crashing down on his skull with tragic results. Thankfully, the guardian angel was on duty that day!

Several years later, another scenario played itself out. On Jack's eighteenth birthday, he enlisted in the Canadian Armed Forces and travelled to a camp for basic training. Upon arrival, Jack met all the other new members in the platoon. Once they established a camaraderie, the group became part of a close-knit family. One Sunday afternoon, Jack and his buddies drove down to the local beach near the military camp.

It was a warm and pleasant day. As the temperature climbed that afternoon, three of his friends went in for a swim. Others, who had no bathing suits, remained in the car, chatting. Having put on a bathing suit before leaving the barracks, Jack quickly slipped out of his clothes and waded into the water. Since Jack was a weak swimmer, he usually explored the water's depth first. He would determine the distance he could safely swim while still being able to touch the bottom when he stood up so his head would be above the water. On this occasion, he swam away from the shore but neglected first to determine this safe distance.

He swam a short distance from shore, unaware of a sharp drop in the landscape beneath. He stopped, thinking this was safe enough. However, when he tried reaching for the bottom with his feet, he suddenly realized it was much deeper than anticipated. Panicking, he sank. As the water rose over his head, he tried desperately to hold his breath. He knew he couldn't keep it up for long. Feeling this was the end, he extended his hand over his head, hoping it would protrude above the water's surface for others to notice. If his buddies saw him struggling, he knew they would jump in and help. Fortunately, one of his friends observed the raised hand, jumped in and dragged Jack back to safety. The guardian angel must have gone on stress leave after that episode.

Not so! Four years after Jack's stint in the armed forces, he began a new career in education. He had contracted a teaching position at an elementary school forty kilometres from his place of residence. On every trip to work, after turning off the main highway, it was necessary to follow a country road leading to the school. One morning, he glanced into the rearview mirror as he was about to make a left turn onto the side road. In horror, he noticed a vehicle following close behind, signalling to pass on the left.

By law, the passing lane is on the right for those vehicles continuing to their destination on this turn. It was illegal to pass on the left at this junction. However, the car behind Jack was proceeding to pass on the left. Jack slammed on his brakes and waited for the vehicle to pass. As it was moving, he noticed there were six occupants in that car. Had Jack not stopped for them to continue, there would have been a terrible crash. Most occupants of the passing vehicle and Jack could have been severely injured or killed. Jack thanked his guardian angel for being on duty that day, sparing them the unpleasant experience of a tragic situation. Jack does not know how many more years his guardian angel has left before retirement, but he hopes it will be long after Jack's own retirement.

In a recent conversation Jack had with an acquaintance on this same topic, she related how her guardian angel had protected her. When she was approximately eight years old, she and a friend played in an abandoned scrapyard where there were several old, incinerated cars wholly rusted. While they were playing, they didn't notice a storm cloud moving in on them. When it began to rain, both girls ran into one of the old cars to avoid getting soaking wet.

As they huddled inside, protected from the rain, she heard a voice saying, "Get out of here now!"

She had no idea where the sound was coming from, but it repeated the same warning several times. She felt a sudden unexplainable urge to run.

Grabbing the other girl by the hand, she shouted, "Let's go!"

Both girls ran out of the car as quickly as they could. Immediately after abandoning their shelter, a bolt of lightning struck the car. Thankfully, the guardian angel was there to protect them from harm.

Jack is confident others can relate to similar stories of how our guardian angels protected us from harm. For the many occasions we escaped injury, guardian angels deserve our prayers. It can be a short prayer every night and every morning to ask them to continue watching over us.

Guardian angel, this I pray,
Be with me always, night and day.
When in danger and in fright,
Keep me always in your sight.
Lend to me your helping hand.
In darkest hours, be my stand.
Calm my nerves of mental strife,
And guide my soul to everlasting life!

It is self-assuring to know that you are never alone, not even in the darkest hour of life. Although invisible to the human eye, there is always an angel to heal and comfort you. You only need to believe. You are a precious soul to your guardian angel, and he will do everything he can for you! Our guardian angels are closer to us than anything except the love of God.

The Inner Voice

Of all the crazy things that can happen in this world, the most bizarre are those caused by one's foolishness. Thank God that stupidity is not punishable by death, yet it still may cause that outcome. Although, occasionally, a course of action may appear unwise, something inside urges one to go on. The following experience is one that John will not forget for many years to come.

One Friday afternoon, after work, John and his wife, Janet, were planning to visit her mother, Sylvia, a recently widowed lady who was left to maintain a bungalow alone in a small village. For Janet, it was a mere three-hour drive to her house. But the trip kept being delayed due to daily care and concerns that took precedence over their plan. However, they were firm; nothing would deter them from postponing their visit other than stormy weather. So, before making the trip, Janet checked the weather channel and happily found the weather forecast promising a mild January weekend. An hour before dusk, Janet and John dressed warmly in parkas and winter boots, jumped into their vehicle, and headed east on a four-lane highway to the city. From there, it was just an hour north on a paved two-lane road from the metropolis.

The road became polished like a mirror from the constant flow of traffic and the beating sun. Cautiously, John proceeded down the main highway to their destination. Driving with care and caution on icy roads was necessary, for any sudden increase in speed would cause the car to fishtail and land them in the ditch. It would have been prudent to postpone the trip until the road was safer to drive. Yet, they carried on.

While proceeding to their destination, the conversation focused on Janet's elderly mother living alone with no family nearby. Both Janet and John agreed to express their concerns for Sylvia's well-being and convince her to move into a nursing home closer to them. However, being a very independent and self-reliant lady, convincing her to give up her independence may prove difficult. So, their argument would need to cover many benefits available to residents of the nursing home.

Janet knew from past experiences with her grandparents that they needed assistance with daily tasks in their declining years. They found it hard to keep up with laundry and other cleaning duties. When they move into the nursing home, the staff takes care of all those needs.

Since most of Sylvia's friends had died, she desperately lacked companionship. Nursing homes have a built-in social network. Incoming residents quickly establish a friendship with their peers. Depression can set in with old age, so keeping the elderly happy and occupied will make them feel at home. The establishment provides meals and snacks to maintain its residents' health. Janet's mother had diabetes, and thus was always careful with her diet. A dietician on staff would make sure everyone was getting the proper nutrients they needed. Should Sylvia become ill, the best part of nursing homes is their skilled health-care services. All these factors, they thought, would appeal to her. If she agreed to go into a nursing home, Janet and John would find a suitable one for her close to them.

As they discussed this topic, just an hour into their drive, the evening sky lit up like a Christmas tree, aglow with bright flashing red and blue lights. Several police cars were blocking traffic on both lanes of the eastbound highway. John presumed an accident was causing the delay. Meanwhile, the caravan of vehicles ahead had stopped, waiting for the traffic controller's motion for them to proceed.

Thirty minutes passed before the highway patrol established an alternate route. The instructions were for traffic to proceed to the intersection, cross over the westbound lanes, and turn right onto the side road. Several kilometres east, the route would merge with the main highway.

While making the detour at the intersection, John noticed that a double-trailered semi had lost control, jackknifed, and blocked eastbound traffic. The intelligent thing would have been to turn the car around and return home. However, an inner voice kept prodding John to take the alternate way and keep going.

As they proceeded down the established course, a half-ton truck they were following strayed off the narrow trail, causing more delays. John and those behind him took a few minutes to push the vehicle back onto the road.

Once back on the main highway, the caravan of traffic flowed freely into the city. Having executed the loop at the bypass, they both hoped the next leg of the journey would go more smoothly. But their hopes soon faded when a police car came screaming by, followed by a fire truck, a rescue vehicle, and an ambulance. *Now what?* they thought. This trip was taking much longer than expected. Only a miracle would prevent further delays in reaching their destination. It was a matter of thirty minutes north from the junction to Sylvia's home. Unfortunately, more holdups occurred.

A short distance along the perimeter, a two-car accident came into view. Again, there was an interruption as the police sorted out the situation. A stretcher was removed from the ambulance and wheeled to one of the mangled vehicles straddling the highway. The medics carefully lifted one of the car's injured occupants onto the stretcher and into the ambulance. Once the patient was adequately secured inside, the van drove off with sirens screaming and lights flashing. Finally, the signal came to proceed cautiously past the accident. John then drove to the junction and turned north.

Five hours after leaving home, John and Janet finally reached their destination. Their safe arrival produced warm greetings and many hugs. Since it was nearing ten o'clock, everyone was tired and ready to turn in for the night.

The following day after breakfast, the family sat around updating each other on the past week's events. Janet and her mother were enjoying each other's company, chatting and sipping coffee, when suddenly there was a lull in the conversation. Janet's mother lowered her head upon the kitchen table where she was sitting without saying a word. Janet became concerned and asked if anything was wrong.

Janet did not receive a response.

So, she called again, "Mom!"

There was no reaction.

She repeatedly called her with emotion, "Mom!"

Still nothing. Janet rushed over and shook her gently. Her mother raised her head off the table with a puzzled look on her face. She appeared confused and could not understand what had just happened. Janet quickly called the ambulance. They arrived within minutes, placed Sylvia on a stretcher, and transported her to the hospital nearby.

The prognosis was that her mother had suffered a heart attack. Had no one been there, she would have died. John was glad he listened to his inner voice and kept driving rather than returning home despite all the setbacks.

When Sylvia was well enough to return home after three days in the hospital, Janet phoned her and mentioned her discussion with John on their last trip. She presented Sylvia with all the benefits they discussed on the journey. So, Sylvia accepted their opinion and chose the nursing home. Since Janet and John were both employed, it would have been trying for Sylvia to be living with them. Typically, the family becomes the caretaker for the elderly, but it is hard to take care of them when you have a career or a family of your own to support. Nursing homes are a great way of providing seniors with the attention they deserve with round the clock service. Sylvia understood this and agreed.

Within weeks, they located a nursing home nearby to where Janet and John lived. Sylvia accepted the change gracefully. Perhaps she realized that with age comes a loss of energy and movement. In her new residence, she lived peacefully and happily until God called her home at ninety.

Life is a learning experience. We all make mistakes and deserve a second chance. However, it's how we learn from our mistakes that matters. For John, the mistakes he made in life were plenty. But the lessons he learned from those mistakes resulted in him making fewer and fewer of them. That's because he listened more closely to that inner voice, which originates from the heart. To overcome our fears, we must listen to our inner voice. It is never wrong!

Political Aspirations

Money has great power but pales in comparison to political power. Although the leader of the Liberal party lives in prosperity, his political power wanes under a minority government. To regain a majority government, the leader called an election two years early. As we near the end of a political campaign, each political leader dwells on the imperfections and faults of the ruling party. Opposition leaders highlighted the Liberal errors during their power in office to gain points and more significant support for their party. Blood-spilling becomes a power grab. Yet, in a democracy, leaders should demonstrate tolerance and respect for the opposition. Truth should be a politician's objective. They are all working for the good of the country and its people. Yet, many people turn up their noses at politics because political leaders make outlandish promises that winners never fulfill, and losers don't care.

Each party governs with its philosophical aims. The Liberal party maximizes self-rule and political freedom, emphasizing free association, freedom of choice, individualism, and voluntary association. The Progressive Conservatives favour changes in the existing system by social progression through transformations. The New Democratic Party emphasizes positive rights that people may have certain things. The government must create the conditions in which people can achieve these things.

For a teenager of fourteen, the different philosophies between existing political parties did not impact his choices. Although Jeffery could not vote in an election until he turned eighteen, his interest in politics came from his father long before that. Paul was an ardent Progressive Conservative and a mayor of a town of five thousand inhabitants.

Jeff was impressed with the way people respected his father and how he controlled the town. He hoped one day to follow in his father's footsteps. So, to display his eagerness to pursue a political career, his first field of action came when the prime minister called a federal election.

The incumbent asked Jeffery to distribute pamphlets to the citizens in his riding, outlining the party's promises if elected. Jeff jumped at the chance to promote the party of his father's choosing. He got on his bicycle and paddled to every home in town, knocking on doors, ringing doorbells, and handing out pamphlets to those who came to the door. Jeffery was amazed at the residents' kindness when they assured Jeffery that they would vote for the party he was representing.

The Conservative party won the election that year with a landslide and a majority in parliament. The results of the victory so elated Jeffery as he felt his efforts had made a difference. Once bitten with success, he wanted more. Jeff felt ready to move forward. He wanted his friends to join him in his glory, so he asked them to form a club. After some coaxing, they called it the Young Progressive Conservative club or the YPC club.

Initially, thirty members formed the club, but eventually, twenty more joined a cohesive union. The members elected Jeffery as president of the club. Jeff's father and a lawyer in town both agreed to help by subsidizing any expenditures incurred by the club. At meetings, an invited speaker presented their political views and the problems confronting society.

To make the organization more viable, Jeffery proposed holding a dance at the local hall for the community's residents. The proceeds would defray the cost of the hall rental and the orchestra. The club agreed to donate whatever remained to a local charity.

To add frosting to the cake, Jeff received an invitation to attend a mock parliament in Ottawa one day. A mock parliament, or youth parliament, is a simulated learning experience of the parliamentary proceedings for a legislature or other deliberative assembly. Participants play the role of prominent members of parliament, ministers, and speaker, and then they discuss the country's issues in scheduled sessions. Mock parliaments serve as an educational tool to promote understanding of the government's workings. Those in charge of the sessions schedule it for the first week in March.

It was early spring, the time of year when inclement weather could affect many social and business functions, and it did. Jeffery and his father left home in good weather and drove to the airport to catch a plane for Ottawa. As they neared the city, the weather changed abruptly. Much to his disappointment, a call came informing his father that a severe snowstorm and strong winds grounded the aircraft until further notice. The two returned home, deeply disappointed. Jeffery missed a chance of a lifetime to experience the workings of parliament. But that only encouraged him to pursue a career in politics more passionately.

When they arrived home that afternoon, his father tried to lift his son's spirits. Paul advised his son to continue with his studies and work toward a law degree at the university.

When he graduated, and there was a federal election, Paul would try to persuade the leader to present Jeffery as the candidate for this riding. So, Jeff buckled down and soon received the LLB degree.

During his years at the university, Jeff wondered what type of character is necessary to be an excellent leader to so many people. There are good leaders and bad leaders in organizations and businesses. But, to achieve success rather than failure, good qualities of character are necessary. Jeffery felt that integrity should be high on the list of positive attributes. This quality of integrity made sense because if a leader lacks honesty, he should not expect his followers to be honest. Without ethics, success turns into failure. Jeff always held on to truth and honesty throughout his formative years, even though it may have gotten him grounded several times.

Jeff believed accountability stood as another factor of a good leader. He noticed that in dealing with the public, his father had his share of criticisms but fewer expressions of praise for his work. No matter how he tried to please everyone, there was always someone dissatisfied with his decisions. Belonging to a particular party meant rivalry and criticism.

While thinking about his father's promise to make him a candidate for the next election, his mind wandered to the problems in the country. Was he ready to tackle those colossal issues of poverty, racism, drug problems, a lagging economy, and global warming that exist in the country? Some of these problems had existed for many years and were still unresolved. It would take a higher power than a mere mortal to solve these problems successfully. How could Jeff lead his followers into another failure? He would be achieving this career, if elected, mainly for pride and not for leading the people into prosperity. When Jeff carved a career for himself, he wondered if it was for the right reason.

When Jeff asked some of his father's politician friends why they pursued a political career, the replies were varied. One wanted to help people and felt he could accomplish it through politics. Another said he went into politics because it offered him a path to fame and fortune. A third person said politics gave him power and made him feel important. Jeff's father said he went into politics because of his family's expectations, and that also became the reason why Jeff's father tried to steer his son in that same direction.

After hearing why men and women pursued a political career, helping people appealed strongly to him. Jeff knew many professions and occupations provided this same result but on a more personal nature. No one questioned doctors, nurses, police officers and firefighters about their importance, for they made a difference. That aspect of a career choice stood out significantly.

When graduation came, and Jeff received his scroll with the law degree, he told his father he wished to pursue a career in a discipline that would permit him to help people individually. He didn't want to attempt to resolve the daunting and seemingly unsolvable problems of the world. He would prefer to direct his efforts in a more meaningful manner.

Jeff's father felt disappointed in seeing his son abandon a career in politics, but Paul wanted his son to be happy in his work. He saw too many unhappy employees perform their duties grudgingly and tardily. They would come to work in a sombre mood and leave in a similar tone at the end of their shift. Those who enjoyed what they did, gave their best, performed admirably, and looked forward to another day at work.

Jeff took some time after graduation to try something different. He enjoyed and missed the research aspect of obtaining his LLB, and now considered getting a degree in another discipline. Finding the right path remained his own choice now.

One day, a friend of his in the arts field jokingly said to him, "What do you call five thousand dead lawyers at the bottom of the ocean? A good start!"

With the many jokes circulating about the law profession, to practice as a lawyer had minimal appeal to him. Although his father suggested choosing law as the path to a political career, he now abandoned it.

Before proceeding toward an advanced degree befitting his alternative career choice, Jeff checked to see what opportunities presented themselves with his qualifications. The Royal Canadian Mounted Police detachment services required an assistant in a remote northern region of the country. The work entailed dealing with occasional exposure to intoxicated, mentally unstable, hostile, and potentially violent individuals as well as victims of crime and relatives of accident victims who may be distraught. That did not appear to be an exciting field of endeavour. So, he kept looking.

Jeff noted many law graduates pursued a career in politics as elected officials or as support members. The occupation involved policy development, speech writing, public relations, and a range of other activities. Many skills acquired during a law degree proved helpful in public speaking, problem-solving, and analyzing legislation and its effectiveness. This action helped only one individual. He wanted to help many individuals.

Jeff felt the psychiatric profession would fulfill his vocation dream to the nth degree. He could help many individuals who came seeking his advice. Mental health had become a pressing issue in the region since the Covid-19 pandemic struck. But it meant spending at least twelve years in training before setting up his practice. It seemed like a lifetime of schooling to him.

One day, as Jeff lazed around the home, still unemployed and undecided on his career path, there came a knock at the front door. The two police officers stood there bearing sad news. His father had sustained multiple injuries in an automobile accident, and the ambulance had transported him to the local hospital. Jeff and his mother rushed down to the hospital, but they were too late. Paul had succumbed to his injuries. The shock of Paul's passing devastated Jeff and his mother.

Jeff's career problem no longer mattered. The greatest tragedy in life is when one believes the only thing that matters is your own life. Jeff now faced the reality of supporting his mother and himself. To survive, he would have to find the strength and energy to go on when tragedy strikes.

After the funeral, Jeff faced the problem of employment. His father no longer provided for him and his mother. Meanwhile, the town no longer had a mayor to run the city. In most council-mayor systems, the voters directly vote for the mayor. In this town, however, electing a mayor rested in the hands of the council members.

The council members invited Jeff to a meeting at the town hall one day and asked him to consider running for mayor. They lauded praises on his father and the excellent way he handled that position. The council heard about Jeff's education and qualifications, knowledge of the town, and respect from the community. They convinced Jeff he would make an ideal candidate for the position. After four years, they must elect a new mayor. They assured Jeff that this position served as a stepping-stone to more lucrative jobs in provincial politics.

To accept the position without compromising his ethics, he convinced himself he could turn the power given to him into a personal sacrifice by using his knowledge of the law to protect his community from fraudsters and scammers.

When Jeff sat in the mayor's chair, he acknowledged everyone who came to him with a problem and did his best to resolve it. For this, he became the most popular mayor the town ever had, second only to his father.

After serving four years as mayor, he entered the regional arena as a member of the legislative assembly. He served in this capacity for his home riding until he retired. Jeff wanted to be important in life and leave a legacy. Before God called him home, he applauded receiving the career through divine intervention.

CONNECTION

Preordained Destiny

The house next door remained vacant for nearly a year. Nothing much happened around the house. Occasionally, someone would come in, check it over and then leave. This surveillance became necessary to satisfy the insurance company that the house was under someone's care.

Several times a month, two real estate agents from rival companies arrived to show the house to prospective buyers. Otherwise, the house sat vacant, quiet, and lonely each day. However, a change was imminent when someone made a reasonable offer and bought the house.

When the agent completed all the paperwork, there was much action around the building. First, a vintage car drove up the driveway and parked. A middle-aged man, presumably in his fifties, stepped out of the car and unlocked the front door. Soon after, a moving van arrived, and movers hauled in the furniture. Then the utility men came to check the hydro, water, and phone. After everyone left, the car in the driveway remained. Its presence indicated that the owner of the vehicle was occupying this house.

Many retired couples who lived in this quiet neighbourhood preferred to keep to themselves. Bernie lived in this locality for many years and knew most of the people living here. After several weeks, Bernie's new neighbour, who had just purchased the house next door, was no different. He seemed somewhat of a recluse. When anyone passed him on the street with a greeting, he would nod his head and quickly walk away. But Bernie was eager to meet his new neighbour despite the man's aloofness.

One day, an opportunity arose. A strange barking sound emanated from a maple tree in the new neighbour's backyard. The noise aroused Bernie's curiosity, whereby he had to ask himself, *what is a dog doing up in a maple tree?*

To preserve his sanity, he was determined to find the cause of this conundrum. It was not so much the barking that was odd, but the location from where the noise seemed to emanate. The barking would start, and after a few sharp barks, it would stop. The sound was not loud enough to keep the neighbours awake but annoying to those living next door. Somehow, Bernie needed to talk to his neighbour. Bernie would attempt to strike up a conversation with this man at the next opportune moment and inquire about the mysterious barking in his tree.

The next day, when his neighbour returned from the grocery store, Bernie approached and asked if he would spare two minutes of his time. Reluctantly, he complied. As Bernie introduced himself, the man's eyes were diverted to the pavement to avoid eye contact. Following the introduction, his eyes lifted, and he looked directly at the man speaking to him. As the man's shyness waned, the neighbour introduced himself as Malcolm Grimes. Since he was partially hard of hearing, Malcolm asked Bernie to talk a little louder.

Raising his voice to a comfortable level, Bernie inquired about the barking sound coming from the maple tree in his backyard. The news piqued Malcolm's interest, but a puzzled expression formed on his weathered face. Bernie explained that the source of the strange barking sound appeared to come from his maple tree for the past two days. Being hearing-impaired, Malcolm was unaware of this oddity. But he suggested if Bernie wanted to placate his curiosity, he could check it out; Malcolm would provide a ladder.

They proceeded to the back of his house and entered a pristine backyard. The owner retrieved the ladder from the garden shed and propped it up against the tree. Then it was a matter of waiting for the strange sound to begin. After several minutes, a stiff breeze rustled the leaves, and the barking started.

"Woof, woof, woof!"

There did not appear to be any animal perched on the limbs. On closer inspection, the sound was coming from a strange unidentifiable object dangling from a branch. While Malcolm steadied the ladder, Bernie began the climb to retrieve the item. It appeared to be a dog collar equipped with a small battery and a shiny miniature speaker. The moment he gave it a fair shake, they heard that familiar barking sound. The barking stopped when the agitation stopped. The neighbour appeared bewildered by the strange apparatus. Malcolm had never laid eyes on anything like it before and wondered how it ended up in his tree.

Bernie was also unfamiliar with the strange collar and its purpose. He later discovered that the object making the barking sound was an abandoned dog collar used as a device to warn passersby of a dog's presence.

The collar belonged to Blaze, a dog now owned by a family in the next block. The family adopted Blaze from a local dog rescue shelter. Bernie recalled the owner telling him that his dog could not bark and what had caused this vocal malfunction. He explained that Blaze had been debarked at a puppy mill and later adopted by an uncaring family. After being rescued by the animal shelter from that abusive family, a loving couple offered the dog a safe home. He indicated that the animal's maltreatment in the past had made it bitter and warned Bernie not to pet the dog for it might bite. Due to Blaze's disposition, the collar was necessary to warn others of his presence. The owner believed his dog slipped the collar off its neck and left it lying in the gutter, but he had no idea how the object ended up in a tree.

It was common knowledge that several crows nested in the neighbours' trees in this quiet suburb of the city. Crows are very investigative and curious birds. In their first and second years, young crows often "play" with things that are not edible. While scavenging for food, a young crow had possibly picked up the collar and flew off with it.

Presumably, the collar was dangling from the crow's beak as it ascended into the air. The motion would have caused the unit to activate the sensor and produce that familiar barking sound. The noise had probably startled the crow, causing it to release the object from its beak. As the gadget plummeted to earth, it found its resting place in Malcolm's maple tree. Whenever a powerful breeze blew, it shook the branch on which the collar rested, and the barking resumed.

The next time Bernie met his next-door neighbour, he explained the barking collar scenario to him. Malcolm acknowledged that electronic gadgets have always amazed him. With technology progressing so rapidly, he visualized more electronic devices appearing on the market shortly. However, consumers either had not heard about them yet, or the manufacturer had not announced it yet. Bernie agreed with him and noted that some products are so innovative that they can only improve life.

Malcolm offered Bernie a sincere apology for being so aloof, and then kindly invited Bernie to join him for tea.

While enjoying a cup of tea together, they laughed at the invisible dog in the tree. Then Malcolm opened a page of his life and mentioned that his wife had died recently. They had planned to retire and move from the farm into the city. But when Abby, his wife, was diagnosed with inoperable cancer, they withheld the house sale while Abby was undergoing chemotherapy. Unfortunately, the treatment was unsuccessful, and Abby had died. As his eyes clouded with hazy sadness and tears flooded in, he explained how devastated he was when she left him to be with the Lord and how dearly he missed her.

Bernie and his wife became good friends with Malcolm and visited each other frequently. Malcolm was merely an introvert, not a recluse, who preferred minding his own business. The barking dog incident created a lasting friendship, ultimately rescuing a lonely man from unbearable boredom and helping him through the grieving process.

The adage is true: there is no such thing as chance. What seems to us as mere accident springs from the most profound source of destiny. Bernie remains convinced that divine intervention played a part in bringing these two families together.

The Second Fiddle

According to an adage, the early bird always gets the worm. Usually, this is true. Those leading the parade in a smorgasbord queue always pick the choicest desserts in a feeding frenzy. However, that adage does not always apply. Sometimes, the second mouse gets the cheese. While the trap's steel jaws restrain the first mouse, the second mouse relishes the reward. Frank, a senior at a country high school, could attest to this second mouse concept.

Frank lived in a farming community where excitement came at a premium. Occasionally, a fight would break out at the local pub, which would keep tongues wagging for several days. He recalled a recent memory of the most exciting thing that had happened in this town; it kept his community buzzing for weeks.

Several villagers in this small community kept a milking cow for their dairy needs. The town bylaw allowed owners to build a barn on their property for fowl and cows. However, there was nowhere to pasture their cows in the village. Therefore, a local farmer rented part of his farmland for pasture. This piece of grassland was adjacent to the town. In the morning, each man would herd his cow to the field on the outskirts of town. In the evening, each owner would fetch the cow back to his stable. The owners milked their cows by hand and bedded them down for the night. This ritual became a daily routine.

A flurry of excitement arose in this bedroom community one day when someone left the pasture gate open. The entire herd of cattle escaped from the enclosure at midafternoon and paraded down the centre of town. It created quite a stir in the community and took all the available men, primarily seniors, to herd the cattle back to pasture. After school, Frank and the rest of the pupils spent an hour cleaning up the excrement left behind on Main Street in town. That was the last bit of excitement until a new family moved into town.

In elementary school, Frank was a shy lad who had difficulty expressing himself in class. This shyness continued into junior and senior high. His school marks were well above average, but his social life suffered. While his classmates were dating, laughing, talking, going places, having a wonderful time, and enjoying each other's company, Frank would retreat to his home and spend much of his spare time reading library books. The thought of making new friends and dating girls was a stressful undertaking for him. But unbeknownst to him, his life was about to change when a new family arrived in the village.

After the Christmas break, Maggie, a Grade 11 student from a nearby city, appeared in his classroom. Her parents had just moved into the village to establish an automobile repair business. This investment was a golden opportunity for them, as this service was sorely lacking in the community.

Maggie, a tall, slender blonde girl with limpid blue eyes, instantly captured Frank's heart. But knowing his shortcomings, he assumed she would never give him a second look, let alone go out on a date with him. Still, he yearned to talk to her and get to know her better, despite his handicap. Spending leisure time in books had sufficed until then, but somehow things were different now. Mustering up his courage, he was determined to overcome this thorny problem.

From the moment Maggie arrived, most boys in his class were planning to ask her out on a date. At one point, they were taking bets on who would be the first to date her. The competition was intense, and it was annoying to see those boys fawning over her. Yet, Frank hoped he would be the first one to date her. Frank quickly noticed the other boys' advances with Maggie, which spurred him into action.

Despite Frank's limitations, he had strong points going for him. He believed he possessed the virtues of patience, thoughtfulness, and wisdom. Being well-read was a decisive factor too, which would add much to any conversation. These qualities could help build self-confidence and carry him through tough times when swimming against the tide.

The first plan of action was to put aside any forms of jealousy gnawing at him. Psychologists agree that envy comes from a feeling of insecurity and low self-esteem. These feelings are not only detrimental to any relationship but also stifle emotional growth. By suppressing his jealousy, he reasoned that it might be the magic potion that would entice Maggie to go out with him. But if she refused, jealousy would only make him miserable while everyone around him would be unaffected.

He recalled reading an article on this topic, indicating that jealousy is a disease, but love is healthy. The report suggested an immature mind often mistakes one for the other or assumes that the greater the passion, the higher the jealousy! Love and envy are almost incompatible; one emotion hardly leaves room for the other. If both are present simultaneously, they can produce unbearable turmoil! Frank kept that bit of wisdom indelibly etched in his mind. His lack of knowledge about dating was deplorable and needed upgrading.

Searching through the school library for a book on the Dalai Lama several months ago, he vaguely recalled having come across a book on dating. He had flipped through the pages casually and turned it over on its back, but he found nothing of interest on the jacket. He put it back on the shelf, never giving it a second thought. Now, however, there was a desperate and robust desire to locate it. He hoped the book would offer some guidance in overcoming shyness and self-consciousness. The goal was to feel relaxed and comfortable with Maggie.

From his research, he noted that girls mature faster than boys and are thus ready to date sooner than boys too. Perhaps Maggie already had many dates and was now more particular about whom she dated. *What chance do I have of being noticed? And is there perhaps less of a chance of her dating a novice?* he wondered. The answer to his question would come soon.

The student council at Frank's high school got together after class to plan a social evening. The students discussed holding a Valentine dance in the gymnasium on the evening of February 14. After ironing out the logistics of the social event, the principal gave his approval.

When the class got wind of the upcoming event, the rest of the boys were betting on who would be the lucky one to score a date with Maggie to the dance. Unknown to the other boys, Frank was quietly designing his strategy to put into action.

Frank knew if anything represented romance, it was a red rose. In the book of love entitled *Romeo and Juliet*, Shakespeare alluded to the flower as a symbol of love and dating. Frank would go out on a limb and do one better. First, he found a

Valentine card with a beautiful red rose emblazoned on the front. Then, he spent a considerable length of time working on this romantic poem:

A Single Red Rose

From a nosegay of sweet-scented roses
A bloom in the garden of rhyme,
I plucked the loveliest one of them all,
To offer my sweet Valentine!

A single red rose on a slender green stem
Mid-foliage, glistening with dew—
A symbol of love so yearning within,
For someone as precious as you.

This red rose imbued with fragrant perfume
With petals quite fragile and fair,
Comes with a heart I offer to you.
Please handle with ardour and care!

Should you discover the rose, I impart
Does one day just whither and slake,
Yet my love will endure the test of time,
This promise I solemnly make.

—Frank

The next step was to find out where she lived. Frank knew her last name from school and her father's name from a receipt his father received for a recent car repair job. Frank searched in the phone book for her address. Since there was home delivery of mail in the town, he copied that address onto the envelope and inserted the poem in the card with the question, "Would you be my date for the Valentine dance?" Frank felt confident with putting words on paper but awkward when speaking to girls.

After addressing, sealing, and stamping the envelope, he pasted a heart sticker on the flap as a final touch. He rushed over to the post office and dropped it in the letter bin. Now it was just a matter of time waiting for the response, whatever that would be. Frank was confident that all his efforts would achieve positive results; otherwise, he would be crushed and humiliated.

Two days later, on Saturday afternoon, there was a knock at the door. Frank's father opened it, and there stood Maggie, the love of his life, in living colour! She introduced herself and asked to speak to Frank.

When Frank came to the door, seeing Maggie caught him by surprise, and he stammered for something to say.

He wanted to look cool and gallant to her, but as they stood face to face, all he could get out was a frail, "Hi!"

Standing next to him, Maggie noticed Frank was two inches taller than her. Frank, who towered at almost six feet in height, was the tallest boy in his class. Maggie was modestly dressed, neat, and well-groomed. Mustering up enough confidence, he kindly invited her in.

After entering, they proceeded to his father's den. Frank closed the door and motioned for her to sit in the easy chair. Comfortably nestled in his father's swivel chair, he turned to face her. Being a nervous sort, Frank hoped that the swivelling movement of the chair would somehow dispel some of that anxiety. He recalled reading an article about an orator who liked to teeter when speaking to an audience to dispel the nervousness.

For days, Frank had been rehearsing what he would say to Maggie if they were ever alone. At first, Maggie carried the conversation until Frank appeared comfortable with her presence. When the nervousness dissipated, she thanked him for the beautiful Valentine's card and the romantic poem. It had impressed her immensely, and she believed the composition involved considerable effort on Frank's part. She then shifted the conversation to the portion of the Valentine card that asked the question, "Would you be my date for the Valentine dance?" Frank remained on edge, hoping for a positive reply.

She said, "In response to your question about the Valentine dance, let me say that I am particular with whom I choose to date. My preference is someone considerate and unpretentious in my grade level or perhaps a grade above. I try to avoid boys who are loud and boisterous. Finally, I would want my date to be a bit taller than me. So, yes, Frank! I would love to go to the Valentine dance with you next week."

Having said "yes," Frank gave a long sigh of relief. It felt like a ton of bricks had suddenly been lifted off his shoulders. The words "yes, I will go to the dance with you" were now deeply embedded in his mind and would carry him through until graduation. He wanted to shout it out at the top of his voice for everyone to hear, "WOOO-HOOO! Yes! I am the man!"

What he actually said in a soft, pleasant, and refined voice was, "It will be an honour and a pleasure to be your escort to the dance next week."

When Maggie left, Frank, in his meditation, felt as if he was floating on a cloud. He could imagine the talk in class on Monday when they discovered the outcome of that afternoon's meeting with Maggie! He knew how quickly news travelled in a small community such as his.

True to form, on Monday morning of the following week, his Grade 12 class was buzzing with the news that Frank was Maggie's escort for the dance. They all wondered what magic he had performed to land a date with Maggie, for he was always a bookworm and did not appear interested in dating. Feeling good about himself, Frank reasoned that being the second mouse was not all that bad, mostly when the outcome was in his favour.

As months went by, Frank and Maggie spent much of their spare time together. When June approached, Maggie dropped a bombshell, telling Frank her parents were moving to a city in the neighbouring province. Her uncle had died and left her father a well-established service station and gas bar in the city. Her father felt it was too lucrative an opportunity to pass up. This news devasted Frank, for he was growing fond of Maggie.

He tried to soften the sad news by reasoning that happiness always comes with a measure of darkness. If it weren't for sadness, happiness would lose its meaning. More determined now than ever, Frank would take things as they came and bide his time with patience and calmness even to the day of her departure. But deep down inside, he hoped for a change of mind about their move.

When the last day of classes arrived, a moving van drove up to Maggie's driveway. A bout of sadness suddenly overcame him when reality set in, and Frank realized her departure was imminent.

After the van was loaded and ready to leave, Maggie came over to say goodbye. Her departure became the most challenging time of Frank's young life. He forced himself to suppress his tears, fearing it would portray him as a wimp. But, inside, a massive storm was brewing, with torrential rain flooding his spirits.

Maggie pledged to keep in touch by letter at least once a week after exchanging all the niceties. Had computers been invented then, Skype would have made her absence more tolerable.

By autumn of the following year, Frank was beginning his second year of university. When her letters became less frequent, he felt something was wrong and mentioned it to her. In her last correspondence, Maggie broke the news of her engagement. *After dating for six months, this remarkable man proposed marriage.*

With this devastating punch in the stomach, Frank vowed to remain a bachelor for the rest of his natural life. He felt there would be no one like Maggie. The cliché kept running through his head: Water, water everywhere but not a drop to drink! For thirty years, Frank remained single, following his vow to remain a bachelor.

One day, Frank boarded a plane for Hawaii on his vacation and was assigned a seat next to a lady bound for the same destination. He introduced himself to her and commented on how familiar she looked. When he discovered her name was Maggie, he quickly realized this was the same Maggie he had escorted to the dance many years ago. Suddenly, the world became much brighter.

As they renewed their acquaintance, Maggie mentioned she was now a widow. Her husband had died a year earlier. After his demise, she went into mourning for one year to respect him. Now she was consoling her grief by taking a trip to Hawaii. It was where they planned to go before he took ill and died.

Suddenly, an idea came into his head. There was still an opportunity for them to be together again. She was a widow; he was single. His mind was telling him not to go there, but his heart was egging him on. However, since she had passed him over the first time, perhaps there was a chance it could happen again. He would take it one step at a time and see where this would lead them.

For the next two weeks, they were together, enjoying the warm tropical climate, the public beaches, and the incredible natural waterfalls. The world-renowned dining experience made their time together an earthly paradise.

Yet, Frank sensed that it was not enough for Maggie. It seemed as if she wanted something more, something different, something more passionate and romantic, or perhaps a quiet conversation with just the two of them. Frank made a mistake the first time by not pursuing his heart's desire, and he had learned the lesson well. He knew what he had lost and its value. He would be more careful; a second chance may not occur. Everyone deserves a second chance, although, not for the same mistakes.

As they walked hand in hand along a deserted part of the beach two days before their departure, Frank cautiously inquired about her life in the city. He was curious to know what happened to their relationship. Maggie suggested they go down to the lounge nearby, and she would tell him what happened.

They found a beautiful cozy place near the bar, ordered a glass of wine, and settled back in comfortable chairs. And then all those pent-up emotions came pouring out as if she were still in high school. It all came down to absence. Some say absence makes the heart grow fonder. For her, absence made the heart forget. Since they were so far apart physically, she needed to find a balance between independence and dependence. She needed to develop interests of her own and the ability to enjoy life on her own. Yet, she also required Frank's support and advice. In his absence, she did not pay enough attention to their relationship, neglecting to nurture it to its fruition. For this, she was profoundly sorry and regretted it to this very day.

Frank confessed that his academic studies and summer employment kept his mind occupied during those years. Lack of funds prevented him from making an occasional trip to see her. But now they had found each other again! What would prevent them from picking up where they left off so many years ago?

With tears rolling down her cheeks, she confessed she was not the person she once was. Two years ago, she had undergone a double mastectomy and underwent chemotherapy. Although she was in remission, it could reoccur. Would Frank pursue this relationship further under those conditions, she wondered? Without hesitation, he promised Maggie his undying love for her, and any impediment would not deter him from being together for the rest of their lives.

Frank went to the jewellery store the following day and purchased a diamond engagement ring. On bended knee, he proposed to Maggie, and she accepted. The next day, they boarded the plane for home. After the wedding, they lived happily together for many years.

When Frank died many years later, he had the following epitaph on his tombstone: *I didn't mind playing the supporting actor's role, for, at fifty, the second fiddle part led me to stardom.*

The Long Road to Forgiveness

Some people hold grudges for a short while and then get over them; others carry that cumbersome baggage with them for a long time. The tenacious find it hard to forgive and forget. They see themselves as "poor, poor me" victims and the offenders as slimebags. Little do they realize how much energy one wastes submerged in this stressful and sad endeavour.

Bradley and Sheryll shared the same home with their parents for eighteen years. Bradley was two years older than Sheryll, but they got along amicably as far as brothers and sisters go. They were the only two children; Sheryll always looked up to her brother, and he looked out for her.

When Sheryll got married, she moved to a farm with her husband, who owned a quarter-section of farmland. Bradley also got married, moved to the city, where he found suitable employment. Every Christmas, Easter, and anniversaries, they would see each other at their parents' homes for the festivities.

Soon after getting married, Sheryll gave birth to a daughter and named her Sybil. After Sybil graduated from college and began working as a nurse, she met and fell in love with a radiologist at the same hospital. When Sybil became engaged, an unfortunate incident occurred, plunging Sheryll into anger and despair.

The clash happened at a bridal shower for her daughter. During the party, Sheryll's friend, who was hard of hearing, told her that Bradley's wife, Amanda, made a disparaging remark to her about the celebration, allegedly calling it a "disaster." The word she used was not "disaster" but "blaster," a slang meaning great. Sheryll demanded an apology, but no apology was forthcoming. After the wedding, communications between the two families abruptly ceased.

For twenty years, the two never spoke to each other. Much to his dismay, Bradley could not understand the reason for their dispute. Because of the controversy, Bradley and Amanda did not attend the wedding ceremony or the reception. Perhaps their refusal to present the married couple with a wedding gift was just the last straw that broke the camel's back.

He made several attempts to re-establish dialogue. Each Christmas, Bradley would send his sister a Christmas card but never received one in return. After three years of repeating the same gesture, Bradley gave up that practice. He finally resolved that no matter what he did, her grudge was permanent.

Several years later, while cleaning an old trunk one evening, Bradley came across an old unmailed letter that caught his interest. It read:

> *Dear Sheryll,*
>
> *It has been some time since we spoke. I imagine you will be as surprised to receive this letter as I am astonished writing it. The eerie silence which ruined our family gatherings is bewildering and demoralizing.*

This afternoon, while cleaning up some of my belongings strewn about the house for the past several years, I ran across an old photo album. After flipping through its pages, I came across a picture of you when you were just ten years old. Then just as lightning strikes when least expected, it struck me with the thoughts of the past. I held that wonderful picture of you in my hands with such care as though it were sacred. The memory of the day you saved my life reverberated in my mind repeatedly. A bolt of lightning, out of the blue, struck me, and I collapsed. My eyes clouded with haziness, and tears dropped like rain when I remembered how courageously you ran into the house and screamed with fright as I lay lifeless on the grass. In a panic, mother quickly called the ambulance, and soon, I was on my way to the hospital. Your immediate response brought help when I most needed it. It filled my heart with gratitude.

Every incident we went through in our younger days paraded before me in a logical order. Our fishing trip with dad and the boat ride on the lake was clear and well pronounced. I could feel the motion of the boat as it sailed across to the opposite shore.

The next appearance was the walk with our parents to church on Sundays. I recall how intent and serious you looked when the preacher gave a sermon to all the children in the church about loving your neighbour. You appeared to take in every word he spoke. I recall the determination on your face when he asked us if we ever fought with our brothers and sisters. In embarrassment, everyone else said, "yes," but you replied in the loudest voice, "NO!"

When the children were teasing you at school and on the way home, I walked home with you for the entire school year until the teasing stopped. I strangely recall this now after all these years. Those were the good old days. But time quickly puts an end to all good things and robs us of opportunities.

I am so sad that we have not spoken to each other for so long. I don't understand what grave transgression has precipitated this silence.

Goodbye, my dear sister, and God be with you.

Your brother,

Bradley

The letter had stains on the last page as though tears had embraced it. He carefully refolded the note along the original folds and slipped it into the envelope, now discoloured with age. The envelope had been frayed from opening and reopening it while hesitant to send it. The farm address was unclear, but that did not matter, for Sheryll left no forwarding address when they sold the farm and moved. However, the letter carried an ocean of feelings, the remnants of their childhood together long ago. These thoughts recurred as vividly as though Sheryll were still ten.

They say you cannot turn back time, but Bradley had beaten the game and cheated time of its transitory process. He relived the scenes of his twelfth year of life and would continue to do so until he went to be with the Lord. Bradley was now in his declining years. There was winter in his hair, and fog in his eyes, but forgiveness in his heart. Life is too short to hold a grudge for a long time. He forgave and forgot quickly, and that was the only way to live happily. Above all else, the only way we can embrace God's forgiveness is by forgiving others. He was hoping beyond all hope that his sister would eventually share the same sentiments. He prayed each day she would see the light and release him from this uneasy feeling he had lived with all these years.

One day, Bradley was sitting on a bench along with his cronies in the mall. It was three days before Christmas, and his wife was browsing through the ladies' clothing shops. While they whiled away their time with jokes and current events, a familiar face passed by his bench. Sybil, his niece, thought she recognized her uncle, hesitated for a moment, and continued her walk. Bradley prayed she would stop and talk to him, but he wavered too long in calling her name and missed the opportunity.

After his buddies went home, leaving him alone on the bench, Sybil returned and asked to join her uncle. Bradley could hardly believe his eyes! Was this happening, or was it a dream? An outpouring of sentiment came gushing from his heart as he welcomed Sybil to sit and talk with him. She returned the feelings and sat down next to him.

Wasting no more time, Bradley immediately pressed her to explain the reason her mother had ostracized his whole family. He spoke slowly, feeling his way in order not to cause hurt feelings. Bradley mentioned the sadness the family felt by their isolation from her mother and her husband. As he spoke, he tried to discipline his voice to maintain complete control, but his voice quivered, and she noticed a tear roll down the side of his cheek.

Her voice was soft and eminently reasonable when she finally spoke and said it was so ludicrous that a brother and sister who cared so much for each other in their youth should end up in isolation for so many years. Her uncle vehemently agreed with her and waited for a different response, but none came. Bradley was so distraught with her reply that he neglected to ask her whether her parents lived here in this city. However, that was the extent of her conversation with him, and then she left.

Meanwhile, Bradley's wife, Amanda, had completed her shopping and returned to the bench where she left him an hour ago. Accompanying her were Sybil and Sheryll, talking and laughing as they approached the bench where Bradley was sitting.

Amanda said, "Look who I met at the clothing store today!"

Bradley could hardly believe his eyes. Sheryll had aged and had put on a few kilograms but was still the same sister he remembered. Her voice had a positive quality about it as she explained what had transpired just a short time ago.

She told her brother that Sybil met Amanda earlier and asked her to have coffee at the food court. There they intentionally met up with Sheryll and rehashed the whole bridal shower incident the way it had happened as well as their absence at the wedding. Both Amanda and Sheryll were most apologetic about the terrible turn of events and embraced each other lovingly. She had one more important thing to fix, and that was with her brother.

She then approached the bench where her brother was reclining and said, "Give me a hug!"

Bradley stood up, and they held each other for what seemed like an hour.

"Are we good now?" she asked.

Bradley choked up and could not speak. He just nodded his head in agreement.

Christmas is a time for miracles, and this was a miracle that Bradley would cherish. He believed in miracles and knows that they happen. It's all a matter of time.

The Gift That Gave Back

Receiving an unexpected gift from someone you love can conjure satisfying emotions for both the giver and the receiver. Is there anything more gratifying than giving the perfect gift to someone dear to you, someone who will appreciate and treasure it? Kenny was about to discover the truth of that adage one glorious Christmas morning. This road to his enlightenment began in the latter part of August, just four months before Christmas.

One cool August evening, a couple of months before their vacation, Kenny and his wife Veronica spent several hours planning their trip to Whistler, British Columbia. This tourist attraction is considered home to North America's largest ski resort and a year-round mountain playground. By driving at the maximum allowable speed, the journey would take approximately two full days.

The night before their departure, they packed their suitcases for the journey. At six o'clock the following morning, it took just several minutes to pack their ablution necessities, load the luggage into the vehicle, and secure the house.

The drive across the prairies was tedious and uneventful. The scenery passing by was dreary as the kilometres rolled endlessly on. It being autumn, the bare bones of the trees were showing. Since this was a two-day trip, after driving fourteen hours, they found a comfortable motel to rest for the night.

Arriving in Whistler the following evening, they checked into their resort booked several months before departure. It was necessary to reserve accommodations ahead for such a choice tourist location.

The accommodations were luxurious, the cuisine superb, and the atmosphere heavenly. They spent three days just relaxing, resting, and recuperating after the long, tedious journey. They designated the fourth day for shopping.

There were many small shops in the heart of town. Kenny and Veronica patronized and browsed through them all. Strolling languidly along the avenue that afternoon, they came upon a women's clothing boutique nestled conveniently near the main entrance of a shopping plaza.

Suddenly, Veronica felt a strange and uncontrollable urge to step inside and check it out. After several minutes of browsing, her eyes focused on a short, luxurious mink jacket. The light-brown sable cuffs and collar made the dark colour of the fur stand out beautifully. It was love at first sight! Without hesitation, Veronica inquired about the cost. The salesperson assured her the jacket was on sale, substantially reduced in price. In trying on the coat, she discovered it fit her perfectly, as though the manufacturers made it specifically for her. However, there was only one problem—the coat had fabric on the reverse side. The material extended visibly beyond the sleeves when worn on the mink side, giving it an unattractive appearance.

The salesclerk offered to have it altered to hide the fabric. But, when the jacket returned from the tailor shop after the alterations, the material was still visible beyond the cuffs. The seamstress refused to shorten it further, fearing it may destroy the integrity of the coat. Veronica grew circumspect and debated whether to make the purchase or leave it.

For the remainder of their stay at the resort, Veronica would return to the shop several times and try on the mink coat. Each time she tried it on, Kenny would assure her that it looked fine. Yet there was some hesitation, for Veronica always strove for perfection. She always dressed meticulously, with her hair styled perfectly to match the richness of her clothes. This slight oddity in the coat became problematic for her.

On the last day of their vacation, Kenny made a final attempt in persuading her to buy the jacket. However, Veronica would not purchase the jacket despite the salesperson's and Kenny's sales efforts.

The following morning, the couple departed Whistler without the coat. Three hours into their trip, they reminisced about their vacation but avoided the coat episode. After they arrived home, she made no further mention of the jacket.

With the days now growing shorter and the winter solstice approaching, Veronica soon forgot about the mink. November quickly turned into December. Kenny suddenly realized Christmas was just a few weeks away. Searching for a gift the day before Christmas was his usual tradition, a typical masculine behaviour. He finally realized such a practice was not only running against the tide of social custom, but also displayed little about his love for his wife. He must consider finding a Christmas present for Veronica long before the last day of shopping. Even though he dreaded the thought of parading through the busy malls searching for it, he would endure the effort for her sake.

Kenny noticed that some of his golf friends had different opinions about Christmas shopping. Some were ambivalent, while others dreaded the thought of pushing through the crowds. Their abhorrence for shopping was not meant as a sign of disrespect for their wives. Their dilemma was in not knowing what to buy their significant other. The casual hints they may have received from their wives throughout the year seemed to have gone unnoticed. And the mere thought of walking into a lingerie shop for a gift made them highly uncomfortable.

When men discuss the topic of shopping with their wives, it is typical to speak about women's shopping habits. She usually sees something in a shop and tries it on but doesn't buy it. She goes from the first shop to the second and third shop, looking at alternatives and then purchases the item from the first shop. During the Christmas shopping season, that first shop looks like a bomb hit it, doubling their husband's annoyance.

During a shopping trip, a man's concentration is terrible at the best of times. So, he is unsure what to say when his wife asks, "What do you think about this gift?" Questions such as "Will this vase match our couch?" or "Do you think these skates will go on sale in January?" or "Does any other store carry this item?" are useless because the men have no idea how to respond.

Several days before the holidays, Kenny recalled an anecdote about Christmas shopping, and he shared it with his friends.

He said, "Two men went sailing while their wives went Christmas shopping. While they were out in the boat, a terrible storm arose. The water became choppy, and they had a hard time keeping the boat under control. As they steered toward land, they hit a sandbar. They jumped out of the boat, pushing and shoving to dislodge the boat out of the sandbar. As the waves bounced them against the side of the boat, their hair blowing wildly in the wind, one man said with a smile on his face, 'This sure beats Christmas shopping, doesn't it?'"

Kenny's friends exploded with laughter and nodded their heads in agreement.

Then a fantastic idea popped into his head. It suddenly dawned on Kenny that here was an excellent opportunity to avoid the malls at this busy time. The ideal gift was right in front of him. He thought about the mink coat and was thankful that Veronica did not buy the jacket earlier.

Kenny intended to secretly purchase the jacket and have it sent to him without Veronica's knowledge. He wondered whether the jacket was still available after all this time. And, if it was, how could Kenny get it into the house without Veronica's knowledge? He wanted to make her gift a total surprise.

Conveniently, Veronica was employed and away from home during the day. So, he called the owner of the boutique and enquired about the jacket.

"Yes, it is still available," she affirmed.

The salesclerk had a vivid recollection of Veronica and her many visits to the shop. Their frequent meetings had placed them both on a first-name basis by the time of her departure. The lady also remembered Kenny standing by the shop door and waiting patiently.

After the transaction, the manageress indicated she would send it by courier to the address he provided. Assured that the plan was now in progress, he hoped the rest of his strategy would go smoothly.

A few days following the purchase, Kenny arrived home from an errand and was alarmed to discover a package sitting on his doorstep.

The courier's actions appalled Kenny for leaving an expensive parcel unattended outdoors! Anyone could have come along and stolen the box! Thankfully, he arrived home early that day. He brought the gift into the house, wrapped it in colourful Christmas paper, and concealed it in an empty Christmas tree container in the storage room. There it remained until Christmas morning.

Kenny learned from experience that an excellent way to approach gift giving is by its presentation. A unique presentation can make a gift simply perfect. With a bit of imagination and creative thinking, an ordinary present can be made extraordinary. Since this was no ordinary gift, a unique presentation would significantly affect the recipient. Employing creative thinking, Kenny placed a small fake present under the tree to serve as a decoy.

After returning home from church on Christmas morning, it was time to relax by the fireplace and open the gifts under the tree. The jacket, however, remained hidden in the tree box under the stairs.

When Veronica tore open the bogus gift wrapping, she found three books, temporarily removed from the bookshelf and placed in a box for weight. She did a long, slow slide with her eyes, and her festive mood turned sombre.

Quickly faking embarrassment, Kenny cried, "Oh no, I placed the wrong box under the tree in error!"

He ran back to the tree box and dragged out the wrapped mink jacket. There was an odd mingling of wariness and amusement in Veronica's eyes as she opened the gift. When the lid was flipped open, the mink jacket glowed luxuriously before her eyes.

Taking a quick breath of astonishment, she exclaimed, "Oh my goodness!"

Still, she was afraid to pinch herself lest it was a dream. It was unbelievable—the jacket she loved so much was before her very eyes. Suddenly, tears of joy flooded her eyes and flowed down her face. Impulsively, she jumped up and threw her arms around Kenny. The embrace, it seemed, lasted for an eternity.

A great feeling began to well up in Kenny's soul as he stood in the embrace of his wife. The gift brought him so much joy and satisfaction, mainly because it made Veronica happy. He discovered that giving gifts was more satisfying than receiving them. This gift became a proper recognition of his wife's worthiness, a declaration of her significance, and just another way he could give of himself to her.

Veronica always believed the manufacturer had her in mind when they created the jacket. Now it finally came home! The coat was taken to a furrier and altered to perfection. That perfect gift just kept giving and giving and giving! For the rest of the Christmas season and beyond, both Kenny and Veronica experienced the sunshades of their lives.

An Adventurous Tour of Duty

The night became incredibly dark as the swirl of greasy fog rolled in and obscured the streetlamp directly overhead. Private Phil Hansen, a member of the Canadian Armed Forces, stood directly beneath it, waiting patiently for the next city bus to transport him back to the barracks. The cushioning silence of fog put his mood at ease as he recalled what brought him to this strange city and this point in life.

His first civilian nine-to-five office job in Canada was as appealing as a colonoscopy. Phil was in search of adventure. The commercials on television had led him to believe there was nothing more adventurous and fulfilling than a tour of duty in the armed forces, patriotically serving his country, Canada.

In his research on this career, he discovered that life in the military was more than basic training, going on exercises and deployment. It was also about adventure, programs, services, and protocols that made a career in the armed forces one of a kind.

Phil Hansen, an adolescent who had just turned eighteen, was intrigued by all this hype, enticing young men to come and serve their country. Answering the call became progressively more enticing each day, beckoning and haunting him until he finally gave in. The decision to pursue this path in life was intriguing but risky. The political climate in the south was giving cause for concern. Disputes between the United

States and several rogue nations may have escalated, plunging their northern neighbours and allied countries into military conflict. Enlisting into the Canadian Armed Forces could place Phil at the center of the fray.

Although his father emigrated from Europe, Canada was Phil's country of birth, and he was a true citizen of this land. He was proud to be Canadian, cherishing it as precious and sacred. He would risk his life as a paramedic caring for the sick and wounded.

A further incentive was Phil's aversion to his second menial job as a baker's assistant. The atypical working hours from 5 a.m. to 2 p.m. were crimping his social calendar. The minimum wage provided even less of an enticement to continue this employment. Buttering dough on a conveyor belt and sprinkling it with cinnamon was tedious and highly unchallenging. It was time to explore the world beyond the province he had called home for eighteen years.

He discovered there were many arms of the armed forces, some more appealing than others to him. Upon careful study of the options available, the medical arm was most inviting, for it spoke to his personal pacifist philosophy. It would allow him to travel, provide him with suitable training for a meaningful career, and he would avoid combat.

With the decision to enlist being foremost in his mind, he focused on locating a recruiting centre. The adventure and all the benefits the armed forces offered seemed highly intriguing and worthy of consideration. He envisioned himself as a soldier in the medical division, providing an essential service to his country.

Having no problem locating the office, Phil appeared at the Canadian Armed Forces Recruiting Centre to enlist. He understood that his contract was in effect for three years.

The requirements for acceptance were to complete a battery of written tests and pass a medical and physical exam. When he met all the prerequisites, the Department of National Defence accepted him as a recruit in the branch of his choice.

The first leg of this beautiful journey was a train trip from the city for basic training. Boarding the train and not having to pay for the fare felt odd but strangely gratifying. The federal government was now looking after his travel expenses.

Basic training entailed learning the core skills and the knowledge to succeed in a military environment. It was the most demanding experience Phil had ever encountered, requiring hard work and perseverance. Courses focused on necessary military skills, handling weapons, first aid, and ethical values. Since physical fitness was an essential part of military service, much of the course focused on physical fitness training.

After completing basic training with twenty-five other recruits, Phil's adventure took him to another camp that trained new soldiers. Phil still shudders when recalling an incident that happened one day. The recruits had to camp in tents in the wilderness adjacent to a shooting range. One day, Phil and several of his friends went for a walk across the shooting range after supper, looking for spent ammunition. In their search, Phil found an unexploded mortar shell. Unfamiliar with such weaponry, he picked it up, elated with his discovery, and brought it to the sergeant's tent, expecting platitudes. Phil entered the canvas with the mortar shell, all excited about his find. Before he could ask about its identity, the sergeant's face suddenly turned ashen white.

He let out a bellow of expletives that startled the entire camp. "Get that &*## thing out of here right now!"

Phil made an abrupt about-turn and carefully returned the shell to where he had found it.

After disposing of the mortar, Phil went back to ask the sergeant for information about the weapon and why there was such an urgency to remove it from his tent. The sergeant explained the reason for the speed of abandoning the weapon. He depicted mortar shells as weapons used for close fire support and described them as lightweight, man-portable, and muzzle-loaded. This mortar was an unexploded weapon that had malfunctioned. Any movement may have caused it to explode, killing the handler and everyone around.

That night, Phil had little sleep thinking about what might have happened. He understood why life abounded with tragedies. It finally dawned on him that his life's real tragedy was his lack of spirituality, and this incident was a personal encounter with God.

When training was complete, the recruits returned to base camp and received a posting to a medical unit. Hansen found himself assigned to the Third Field Ambulance as a stretcher-bearer. However, since the Canadian Forces were not engaging in any active military combat at this time, the commanding officer assigned him to the orderly room as an administrative clerk. The position was a blessing beyond all expectations.

When the one-year stint at base camp ended, the Department of National Defence ordered the entire unit to be moved west across three provinces. With their belongings packed, the crew set out for the long, arduous journey in a convoy of military vehicles. Being the youngest man in the group, Hansen rode in the lead vehicle with the commanding officer and driver. With the commanding officer in the lead and all his men following right behind in jeeps, vans and trucks, the unit struck out for their new home.

On their journey to a permanent home, they made a slight detour to take in the summer maneuvers. When the summer games ended, the unit finally arrived at its new home. After the Third Field Ambulance Unit finally settled in their barracks, the army employed Private Hansen as an administrative clerk. However, within six months, much to his surprise and delight, the army posted him overseas for a one-year tour of duty at a British Military Hospital in Germany. The British and the Canadian Medical units worked together, providing medical services to the military stationed in that country.

It was an exhilarating feeling, knowing that a military jet would soon carry Phil to a foreign country he had only read about in books at school. The thought of travelling so far from Canada was somewhat daunting yet still exciting.

Hansen presumed that the trip overseas would be luxurious, somewhat like a ride on a supersonic jet. It was not. The conveyance was a four-propellered cargo plane with bench seats along both sides. The airplane would usually transport military equipment. Just as luck would have it, Hansen found himself seated at a location close to one of the aircraft's wings. This location was a wrong choice; the noise was deafening due to the proximity of the engines.

They were airborne for some time before the plane landed on an island in the Azores for refuelling. The Azores is one of the two autonomous regions of Portugal. It is an archipelago composed of nine volcanic islands in the North Atlantic Ocean, about twenty-five hundred kilometres southeast of Newfoundland, Canada.

After the plane refuelled, it continued to England. After surviving six gruelling hours of flight, they finally approached the first leg of their journey to Germany. From there, their journey continued by train and boat to their destination. When Hansen disembarked at Nottingham, the noise of the engine's hum left an annoying drone in his ears that lasted for several days.

All the passengers on the plane received train passes to continue to their assigned Canadian Forces base in Germany. They took the train from Nottingham to Dover, crossed by ferry to the Hook of Holland, and then took another train to a town in North Rhine-Westphalia, Germany. A van waited for Phil's arrival to transport him to the British Military Hospital. There he would serve as a medical assistant in the hospital.

Although Phil trained as a medical assistant in Canada, this field of endeavour proved intolerable. The antiseptic hospital smell was nauseating. Tending to the sick required patience, a quality sorely lacking in his character makeup. He needed to return to the orderly room and into administration once more.

Rumours had it that the present administrative clerk was about to complete his tour of duty in Europe in just a few days. He was on a three-day pass to England and repatriating to Canada the following week. Upon hearing the good news, Hansen approached the commanding officer and requested reassignment of duties to the orderly room. He argued that the experience he had in the orderly room outweighed the hospital ward's background a hundredfold. The present clerk's repatriation and the lack of an immediate suitable replacement enticed the commanding officer to move Private Hansen to administration, a position he enjoyed immensely.

The onus was on Phil to transport and collect the unit's official mail and the Canadian soldiers' mail stationed at this hospital, along with administrative duties. A German civilian employed by the hospital would bring the minivan to the postal room, pick up the mail clerk, the outgoing mail, and then leave for the main post office thirty kilometres away. It was an enjoyable break from the daily routine of paperwork in the office. Each run was an adventure of its own.

A week before Christmas, the Canadian crew decided that they would like a spruce tree decorated for the holidays. They approached Private Hansen and asked him if he would stop on the way back from the mail run, slip into the woods along the way, and pick one up. He was glad to oblige. However, unbeknownst to him, it was illegal to cut trees in the woods without a permit. When he mentioned the request to the driver, the driver agreed to help.

On the way back from the mail run, the driver noticed a bush in the distance. When they neared the grove of trees, the driver stopped, and they walked into the forest. Finding a suitable specimen, they cut it down and began dragging the tree out of the bush to the minivan. Suddenly, two members of the local constabulary appeared out of nowhere and confronted the duo about the tree. The driver, in his native German, spoke a few words to them. After exchanging civil words, the police officers returned to their patrol car, allowing Phil to bring the tree to the minivan and the barracks.

Several kilometres later, Phil asked the driver what conversation transpired between him and the police officers. They had warned him it was illegal to cut down trees unless one possessed a license for such an undertaking. However, cut and abandoned trees were permissible to take. The driver had informed the police officers that someone had cut the tree and left it. The driver then received permission to move the spruce tree to the van.

The soldiers set up the tree at the hospital barracks and decorated it with Christmas ornaments saved from previous years. That magnificent tree brought the holiday spirit of Christmas to everyone. It eased the loneliness for all who longed to be home with their loved ones in Canada.

Let's get back to the introduction of this story, and the reason that Phil was standing under a streetlight on a foggy night. It happened quite unpredictably. That evening in January, some Canadian servicemen went down to the local pub for some libation. The patrons were leaving as the clock approached closing time. Someone announced that a heavy fog was rolling in and enveloping the town. Due to poor visibility, the highways department did not recommend travel. This unusual situation amazed Phil, for he would never have seen such fog during a Canadian winter.

Hansen's problem now was to return to the barracks under this dense cloud of darkness. Under that streetlamp, the fog was so thick that it made the light virtually invisible. To get to the barracks would mean travelling across town, and no buses were running. Perhaps in the pub, someone lived nearby who could put him up for the night. When he returned to the bar, the server was uncertain why he had come back, and in her broken English, asked Hansen if he was having difficulties getting home. Immediately, there was a sense of belonging when he noticed she had a heavy Russian accent. The conversation quickly switched to Russian, and Hansen explained his problem. He had no difficulty speaking the language, for his mother was Russian, and his father was Anglo-Saxon and fluent in English and Russian.

She introduced herself as Svetlana and indicated she lived nearby. Her husband, Igor, would come by shortly, and they would walk home together. The couple invited Hansen to stay with them for the night. He was thrilled for both the lodgings and the opportunity to converse with them in Russian.

The following morning, Phil thanked the family for their hospitality and returned to the orderly room to resume his regular duties. That evening, rather than returning to the German pub, he spent the evening at the military canteen.

As a diversion from work, the servicemen and women gathered at the British Military Hospital's canteen. After supper every evening, those not on duty would gather at the canteen, drink beer and exchange exciting stories about their daily and weekly work experiences. The social gathering seemed odd. The British and Canadians gathered at the opposite ends of the room. Hansen never discovered why this behaviour persisted throughout Phil's tour at the British Military Hospital.

Although Phil was a Canadian serviceman, he always gravitated toward the British side of the room and conversed with them. A desire to have a better understanding of people from other countries had prompted this association with them. From his involvement with the British, a friendship developed with Taffy from Wales and David from England. Frequently, they would tour the bars in Iserlohn to meet some of the city's local German girls.

When Phil's tour of duty ended in Germany, and the army repatriated him back to Canada, David's friendship continued through letter-writing. Soon, David became engaged to a British nurse in England, and Phil found a wonderful girl in Canada.

Thirty years later, David and his wife, Irene, journeyed to Canada to pay Phil and Zenia a visit. The two couples toured the province and then continued to Western Canada and parts of the United States. It was a delightful reunion. On their return to England, Phil and Zenia presented them with a clock decorated with Easter Eggs mounted on the face.

This fantastic tour of duty brought a better understanding of people and their cultures. Perhaps such an endeavour could prevent hatred amongst people of different ethnic backgrounds and ease world tensions.

When looking upon life as a journey, some say it would be nice to have a preview of it before they embark. They could see where they are going, understand what is out there waiting for them, see the detours, the potholes, and danger spots that lie out there, and plan how to meet them. We could then travel the road confidently, and it would all come together and make sense. But then, it would not be an adventure. It would be dull and mundane, like watching a rerun of a football game. The experience and excitement would be gone. Phil searched for adventure and found it. And man, what a ride!

Teach the Children

When December approaches, all five human senses begin to concentrate on Advent and the celebration of Christmas. This festive season conjures up sights of decorative outdoor lights that turn the yard into a beautiful kaleidoscope of colours. We have visions of candles, stars, wreaths, ornaments, presents, and hollies. Evergreen trees captivate our sense of smell with the scent of pine needles. We can almost hear Santa Claus' reindeer prancing on the rooftop and bells jingling as Santa climbs down the chimney with presents. Recalling the taste of turkey, plum pudding and candy canes causes us to salivate. Some make it a practice to set aside one evening of Advent a year to cruise the residential areas of the city or town they live in and admire the unique displays of Christmas lights. A feeling of magic fills the air as Christmas draws near. But for some, sad to say, the most important reason for celebrating Christmas seems to have been left out of the celebrations—Christ Himself.

When you consider all the work and money that goes into some of those elaborate outdoor Christmas displays, it would be interesting to know how many occupants have seen the inside of a church. Are their efforts all just for show, or are they really and genuinely expressing their love for Christ in their own way through this medium? People have become so caught up in the materialistic aspect of the season that they leave out the real reason for the season. Or do they?

By no means is there anything wrong with adorning our homes with lights, trees, ornaments and all the other festive things that occupy our thoughts during Advent. But they should be placed in their proper perspective. The outward and visible expressions should bear a relationship to the event. You might ask, what then is the relationship between Christ's birthday and lights, ornaments and gift giving?

A connection existed with everything we think about at Christmas, including gift giving. The virtue of giving gifts to others is that it displays our attempt to imitate God the Father humbly, who gave His Son as His gift to us on that first Christmas morning. You may remember that the Magi brought gifts to Christ of gold, frankincense, and myrrh. Presents are nice to give, and they are lovely to receive. But our primary focus should be on the holy season—the birthday of our Lord and Savior Jesus Christ. Parents may use gift giving as a ransom to regain their children's love and respect after months of neglect.

Over the past few years, many email messages have appeared in Cameron's inbox. One such email dealt beautifully with the true meaning of Christmas. The article's theme focused on children and was entitled "Teach the Children." This message said:

> I just finished the household chores for the night and was preparing to go to bed when I heard a noise in the front of the house. I opened the door to the front room, and to my surprise, Santa himself stepped out from behind the Christmas tree.

He placed his finger over my mouth so I wouldn't cry out. "What are you doing?" I asked.

The words choked up in my throat, and I saw he had tears in his eyes. His usual jolly manner was gone. Gone was the eager, boisterous soul we all know.

He then answered me with a simple statement. "Teach the children."

His remark puzzled me. Santa anticipated my question and brought forth a small toy bag from behind the tree with one quick movement.

As I stood bewildered, Santa said, "Teach the children! Teach them the old meaning of Christmas—the meaning that Christmas has forgotten nowadays."

He reached in his bag, pulled out a fir tree, and placed it before the mantle. "Teach the children that the pure green colour of the stately fir tree remains green all year round, depicting the everlasting hope of mankind, and all the needles point heavenward, making it a symbol of man's thoughts turning toward heaven."

He again reached into his bag and pulled out a brilliant star. "Teach the children that the star was the heavenly sign of promises long ago. God promised a Savior for the world, and the star was the sign of fulfillment of His promise."

He then reached into his bag and pulled out a candle. "Teach the children that the candle symbolizes Christ who is the light of the world. When we see this great light, we are reminded of Him who displaces the darkness."

Once again, he reached into his bag, removed a wreath, and placed it on the tree. "Teach the children that the wreath symbolizes the real nature of love. Real love never ceases. Love is one continuous round of affection."

He then pulled out from his bag an ornament of himself. "Teach the children that I, Santa Claus, symbolize the generosity and goodwill we feel during December."

He then brought out a holly leaf. "Teach the children that the holly plant represents immortality. It represents the crown of thorns worn by our Savior. The red represents the blood shed by Him."

Next, he pulled from his bag a gift and said, "Teach the children that God so loved the world that He gave His begotten Son. Thanks be to God for His unspeakable gift. Teach the children that the wise men bowed before the Holy Babe and presented Him with gold, frankincense, and myrrh. Gold was to honour His kingship, frankincense to honour His divinity, and myrrh to honour His humanity as He was destined for death. We should always give gifts in the same spirit of the wise men."

Santa reached into his bag, pulled out a candy cane, and hung it on a tree. "Teach the children that the candy cane represents the shepherd's crook. The crook on the staff helps to bring back stray sheep to the flock. The candy cane is the symbol that we are our brother's keeper."

He reached in again and pulled out an angel. "Teach the children that it was the angels that heralded in the glorious news of the Savior's birth. The angels sang, 'Glory to God in the highest, on earth peace and goodwill toward men.'"

Suddenly, I heard a soft twinkling sound, and from his bag, he pulled out a bell. "Teach the children that as the lost sheep are found by the sound of the bell, it should bring humanity to the fold. The bell symbolizes guidance and return."

Santa looked back and was pleased. He looked back at me, and the twinkle was back in his eyes. He said, "Remember, teach the children the true meaning of Christmas and do not put me in the centre, for I am a humble servant of the

One that is, and I bow down to worship Him, our LORD, our GOD."

The message presented a uniquely excellent way of thinking about Christmas and making it a holy day. If only children and adults celebrated Christmas through the eyes of this Santa Claus.

Children are very perceptive and quickly process and absorb it into their minds. If we provide them with the right building blocks, they will translate themselves into a life of happiness. When you teach children, they form the future generations.

God offered humanity the gift of His own Son; pass that gift on to the children. Tell them the true meaning of Christmas. Please give them a gift that will last for generations, even unto eternity. It's the greatest gift you can give them and the least expensive.

It has been the custom of some families to leave an empty chair at the table when enjoying their Christmas dinner. The empty chair left at the table includes a place for Jesus. In this way, Jesus becomes included in His birthday celebration.

An adage claims, "It is better to give than receive." That saying is true because of the joy and happiness we see in the gift's receiver. We forget about ourselves for a while and find time for others.

About the Author

I, Mike Henry Tkachuk, was born and raised in a small village of Aumsville, in Manitoba, Canada. I attended high school at Major Pratt Collegiate in Russell, Manitoba. I studied at the University of Manitoba, Brandon University, and Ottawa University. I received the following degrees: BA., BEd, M.Ed, and a certificate in Eastern Christian Studies. I hold an Education Administrator's Level II certificate, and a province of Manitoba Teaching Certificate. After serving in the Canadian Armed Forces for four years, both in Canada and abroad, with the Royal Canadian Army Medical Corps, I was employed as a teacher/principal in the elementary and junior high grades. Since graduating from the Catholic Seminary in Ottawa, I have been employed as pastor of St. Mary's Ukrainian Catholic Churches in Brandon and Portage la Prairie, Manitoba. I am married to my wife, Dolores. My first poetry book, *Poetry, My Obsession*, was published in 2011. Another book of poetry entitled *Perspective Reflections in Rhyme* was published in 2018.